Acting Edition

Country Girls

by Stephen Brown

SAMUEL FRENCH

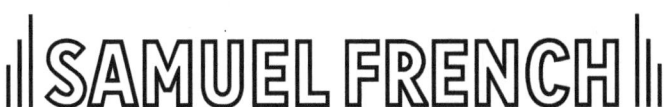

Copyright © 2024 by Stephen Brown
All Rights Reserved

COUNTRY GIRLS is fully protected under the copyright laws of the United States of America, the British Commonwealth, including Canada, and all member countries of the Berne Convention for the Protection of Literary and Artistic Works, the Universal Copyright Convention, and/or the World Trade Organization conforming to the Agreement on Trade Related Aspects of Intellectual Property Rights. All rights, including professional and amateur stage productions, recitation, lecturing, public reading, motion picture, radio broadcasting, television, online/digital production, and the rights of translation into foreign languages are strictly reserved.

ISBN 978-0-573-71093-3

www.concordtheatricals.com
www.concordtheatricals.co.uk

FOR PRODUCTION INQUIRIES

UNITED STATES AND CANADA
info@concordtheatricals.com
1-866-979-0447

UNITED KINGDOM AND EUROPE
licensing@concordtheatricals.co.uk
020-7054-7298

Each title is subject to availability from Concord Theatricals Corp., depending upon country of performance. Please be aware that *COUNTRY GIRLS* may not be licensed by Concord Theatricals Corp. in your territory. Professional and amateur producers should contact the nearest Concord Theatricals Corp. office or licensing partner to verify availability.

CAUTION: Professional and amateur producers are hereby warned that *COUNTRY GIRLS* is subject to a licensing fee. The purchase, renting, lending or use of this book does not constitute a license to perform this title(s), which license must be obtained from Concord Theatricals Corp. prior to any performance. Performance of this title(s) without a license is a violation of federal law and may subject the producer and/or presenter of such performances to civil penalties. Both amateurs and professionals considering a production are strongly advised to apply to the appropriate agent before starting rehearsals, advertising, or booking a theatre. A licensing fee must be paid whether the title(s) is presented for charity or gain and whether or not admission is charged. Professional/Stock licensing fees are quoted upon application to Concord Theatricals Corp.

This work is published by Samuel French, an imprint of Concord Theatricals Corp.

No one shall make any changes in this title(s) for the purpose of production. No part of this book may be reproduced, stored in a retrieval system, scanned, uploaded, or transmitted in any form, by any means, now known or yet to be invented, including mechanical, electronic, digital, photocopying, recording, videotaping, or otherwise, without the prior written permission of the publisher. No one shall share this title(s), or any part of this title(s), through any social media or file hosting websites.

For all inquiries regarding motion picture, television, online/digital and other media rights, please contact Concord Theatricals Corp.

MUSIC AND THIRD-PARTY MATERIALS USE NOTE

Licensees are solely responsible for obtaining formal written permission from copyright owners to use copyrighted music and/or other copyrighted third-party materials (e.g. artworks, logos) in the performance of this play and are strongly cautioned to do so. If no such permission is obtained by the licensee, then the licensee must use only original music and materials that the licensee owns and controls. Licensees are solely responsible and liable for clearances of all third-party copyrighted materials, including without limitation music, and shall indemnify the copyright owners of the play(s) and their licensing agent, Concord Theatricals Corp., against any costs, expenses, losses and liabilities arising from the use of such copyrighted third-party materials by licensees. For music, please contact the appropriate music licensing authority in your territory for the rights to any incidental music.

IMPORTANT BILLING AND CREDIT REQUIREMENTS

If you have obtained performance rights to this title, please refer to your licensing agreement for important billing and credit requirements.

COUNTRY GIRLS was originally produced under the title *Montgomery* by Bristol Valley Theater (Karin Bowersock, Executive Artistic Director) in Naples, NY, and premiered on August 19, 2018. The performance was directed by Karin Bowersock, with scenic design by Jack Golden, lighting design by Christina Watanabe, costume design by Christopher Metzger, sound design by Brandon Reed, and props by Ryan Dziedziech. The production stage manager was Meaghan Finlay. The cast was as follows:

MEGAN . . . . Kalia Lay
KIMMY . . . . Claire Noonen
LARRY . . . . Rick Apicella
CHET . . . . Neil Brown
PATTY . . . . Shannon Haddock
RICK . . . . EJ Cantu

The Southeastern premiere of *Montgomery* was produced by Trustus Theatre (Chad Henderson, Artistic Director) in Columbia, SC, on August 23, 2019. The performance was directed by Sharon Graci, with scenic design by Curtis Smoak, lighting design by Laura Anthony, costume design by Janine McCabe, sound design by Chad Henderson and Daniel Machado, and props by Sam Hetler. The production stage manager was Ginny Ives and the assistant stage manager was Krista Grevas. The cast was as follows:

MEGAN . . . . Cassidy Spencer
KIMMY . . . . Lilly Heidari
LARRY . . . . Kevin Bush
CHET . . . . Gabe Reitemeier
PATTY . . . . Elena Martinez-Vidal
RICK . . . . Jason Stokes

CHARACTERS

MEGAN – 14, female.

KIMMY – 13, female. Megan's best friend.

LARRY – 45, male. A cop.

CHET – 26, male. Larry's partner.

PATTY – 40s or 50s, female. Chief of Police.

RICK – 40s, male. A semi-famous country music singer.

MARY – 40s, female. A semi-famous country music singer and Rick's wife. Heard in voiceover only.

SETTING

Sheepshead County, Texas.

TIME

The Present.

NOTE ON MUSIC

Sheet music for the songs "Star Quality" and "Montgomery," composed by Eliza Simpson, is available for licensing. Please consult your performance license or contact your licensing rep for more information.

Scene One

(**KIMMY** *and* **MEGAN** *are hanging out in Kimmy's room.* **KIMMY** *is sweet and naïve in that way where she still thinks all her dreams will come true if she just tries hard enough. She has a slight lisp, which no one has ever told her about.)*

(**MEGAN** *is the opposite in basically every way. They're best friends.)*

(Go.)

MEGAN. Okay here's the plan.

Part One: The concert starts at 8:30, right? But Rick Montgomery probably won't take the stage until later, so I'm thinking we don't need to be there until about 9:30 or 10.

KIMMY. Got it. Check.

MEGAN. And since we don't actually have any tickets, I'm thinking we'll go in the back way. Security is really lax there.

KIMMY. Lax. Got it. Check.

MEGAN. How many times have you driven your grandma's car?

KIMMY. A couple. But I've only got into one accident so far. And nobody knows about it.

MEGAN. Perfect. So I think we should leave at around 9 after your grandma goes to sleep. Where does she keep her keys?

KIMMY. By the back door, but she knows, so we can go whenever.

(*Beat.*)

MEGAN. You told your grandma?

KIMMY. Oh no, she doesn't care.

MEGAN. Kimmy!

KIMMY. She doesn't care, I swear!

MEGAN. I told you not to tell anyone!

KIMMY. But she's my grandma...

(**MEGAN** *sighs, loudly.*)

KIMMY. Why, what'd you tell your parents?

MEGAN. Larry's working and Brenda's at Astroworld this weekend.

KIMMY. Awww, *lucky!*

(*Wistful.*) I bet she sees some celebrities.

MEGAN. Yeah.

Hey. Did you get the masks?

KIMMY. Oh! Yeah.

You are gonna be so excited.

(**KIMMY** *goes to her sock drawer and pulls out two ski masks. One's purple, the other's blue. It looks like they've been decorated. She's super proud of them.*)

MEGAN. They're supposed to be black.

KIMMY. Yeah but these'll work okay, right?

MEGAN. Did you...decorate them?

KIMMY. Well – only 'cause I used them for my Halloween costumes a couple years ago.

MEGAN. What happened to the money I gave you to buy new ones?

KIMMY. Uuuuuuum.

(Super coy.) I don't remember…

MEGAN. *(Closes her eyes.)* What did you spend it on?

KIMMY. Okay well there's this website online where you can buy celebrities' hair?

MEGAN. *(To herself.)* God damn it.

KIMMY. No hey but listen and so they had some of Madonna's hair on discount for a limited time only.

So.

I mean I couldn't *not* get it.

MEGAN. Why.

KIMMY. The instructions say I'm supposed burn it in a séance, pray to Jesus three times, and it'll heal my vocal cords.

MEGAN. That wasn't Madonna's hair.

KIMMY. Yeah huh. It's blonde. And when you burn it, it smells like sapphire and ivory.

MEGAN. You need to get your head in the game here Kimmy.

KIMMY. My head is in the game.

MEGAN. This is Rick Montgomery's farewell tour. Okay?

After tonight, he'll be *gone*.

There are literally zero other nights we can do this.

You can't do a farewell tour twice. That would be stupid.

KIMMY. My head is 100% in the game.

MEGAN. Good. 'Cause I'm trusting you with one of the most important aspects of tonight's plan. Here:

(MEGAN hands KIMMY a hammer.)

KIMMY. ...Why are we gonna need a hammer?

MEGAN. This is for the final part of the plan.

KIMMY. What's the final part of the plan?

MEGAN. The final part is that after we hide your car.

Sneak past security.

And put on our masks.

We're gonna *break* into Rick Montgomery's trailer.

Steal his 1927 Martin 45 guitar.

And get the fuck back home before anyone notices.

KIMMY. ...Do I have to be in charge of the hammer?

MEGAN. Yes.

Besides, you've got small hands. I don't want you to be defenseless.

KIMMY. Defenseless?

MEGAN. In case we run into trouble. Or security surprises us.

This thing can take down a grown man with one quick swipe to the body.

KIMMY. How do you know that?

MEGAN. *Also.* When we're done?

We're gonna need to fucking smash *everything*.

Anything we don't take? Just go fucking crazy on it with this.

That way when Rick comes back to his trailer and is like "where's my shit?"

He won't know what we took because everything'll be in pieces.

It'll be hilarious. Sound good?

KIMMY. ...Maybe this isn't such a good idea.

(Beat.)

MEGAN. What does that mean?

KIMMY. No, just that –

MEGAN. Of course this is a good idea.

KIMMY. I don't – I mean – you don't feel sorta bad about doin' this to Rick Montgomery?

MEGAN. No.

He's rich and he's an awful human being.

KIMMY. *(Not entirely agreeing.)* Yeah...

MEGAN. He's *awful* Kimmy. Magazines say so. The internet says so.

He comes here every year and ruins our town with his trashy music.

KIMMY. No, I know –

MEGAN. He's a trash person

KIMMY. No, I know but like...you don't feel a little bit bad?

Stealing his wife's guitar?

MEGAN. Why would that make me feel bad?

KIMMY. 'Cause she just died.

MEGAN. And?

KIMMY. And...his wife just died, Megan.

And maybe, maybe he's not prepared to have the only thing left of her taken away as well, you know?

(Short pause.)

MEGAN. I'm sorry, are you like... are you trying to back out on me?

KIMMY. No.

MEGAN. You're totally backing out on me!

KIMMY. No, it's just Mr. Ferguson at school said I'm supposed to voice my concerns about things.

MEGAN. What did you think these masks were for?

What did you think we were gonna do when we broke into his trailer?

KIMMY. I don't know.

Just like, maybe like take some pictures of stuff for our instagram or maybe hang out with him if he wants to hang out and sing songs and stuff.

MEGAN. Okay. You know what?

*(**MEGAN** starts packing up her stuff.)*

If you don't want to follow the plan?

That's fine. You don't have to come.

KIMMY. That's not what I'm saying –

MEGAN. I was gonna go alone anyway. So.

And I figured you probably weren't ready anyway.

KIMMY. I *am* ready!

MEGAN. It's fine. We don't have to be a team on this one.

KIMMY. But I wanna be on your team! The Megan Kimmy Team. "Megimmy."

MEGAN. It's okay, I'm just gonna do it alone.

KIMMY. I was just voicing my concerns I said!

(**KIMMY** *starts crying.*)

(*This is something that happens. A lot.*)

(**MEGAN** *watches her, and softens. She sits down next to her friend.*)

MEGAN. *(Patting her on the leg.)* Okay. Ooookay. I'm sorry.

(**KIMMY** *turns away.*)

Nooo come on, don't be like that.

I'm sorry I said you weren't on my team.

KIMMY. Yeah, what're you doin' that for?

MEGAN. I don't know... *(In a weird voice.)* I'm sorry.

...Come on, stop crying.

KIMMY. *(Lying horribly.)* I'm not, I just got something in my eye.

MEGAN. Hey, you have nothing to be concerned about. Okay? Tonight's gonna be fiiiiine.

We're just gonna drive down there. Break into his trailer. Super casual.

Throw the guitar in our backpacks. And then sell it on Amazon!

He's not even gonna know he lost it.

Doesn't that sound easy?

KIMMY. ...I guess.

MEGAN. And then you're gonna have a whole bunch of money to do stuff with.

What are you gonna do with all that money, huh?

KIMMY. I don't know...

MEGAN. No come on, what are you gonna do with all that money?

KIMMY. Buy some professional singing lessons maybe?

MEGAN. That's right. And then you're gonna be such a good singer.

KIMMY. And maybe audition for *The Voice*?

MEGAN. And maybe audition for *The Voice*, exactly.

KIMMY. *(Smiles.)* Okay.

    (**MEGAN** *checks her watch.*)

MEGAN. We should probably head out early. Scope out the area.

KIMMY. Okay.

And but – hey. Do you think maybe…maybe *you* could be in charge of the hammer?

MEGAN. Well. You're either in charge of the hammer or you're in charge of this.

    (She pulls out a Molotov cocktail.)

KIMMY. Whoa! Is that real?

MEGAN. God damn right this is real.

This is what I call the last resort.

Like, in case Rick is in there and we need to cause a distraction to cover our getaway.

KIMMY. I thought he was gonna be doin' his show.

You said we weren't supposed to see him.

MEGAN. You never know.

KIMMY. *(So excited.)* Oh my God, are we going to get to meet him?!

MEGAN. No Kimmy, it's just in case.

KIMMY. Oh my God! Oh my God! *(Pause.)* Oh my God! Do I look okay?

MEGAN. Kimmy we're not gonna see him!

KIMMY. Oh my God but what if we do.

Oh my God what if we freak him out so bad that he *wrote a song about it?!*

MEGAN. Ew.

KIMMY. Like you know that song that's like, "You're so vain, you probably think this song is about you." This song would actually be about us!

MEGAN. We're not gonna see him. Okay?

This is an airtight plan.

KIMMY. *(Wistful.)* Yeah...

MEGAN. *(Darkening.)* ...But I will tell you right now. If we do?

If we do see Rick Montgomery?

He will fucking rue the fucking day he ever crossed us.

*(**MEGAN** throws the hammer to **KIMMY**.)*

KIMMY. This is gonna be so much fun!

(Hard blackout.)

Scene Two

*(Two cops at a crime scene. **LARRY** is giving a speech while his partner **CHET** films him with a bodycam)*

CHET. Aaaaaaand *action*.

LARRY. At approximately 10:46 in the PM tonight, two young teenage females broke into Rick Montgomery's trailer right / before –

CHET. Wait do that, do that again.

LARRY. Wh– uh, which part?

CHET. That part that – Where you were like, "the two girls *broke into* the," you know?

Punch the words this time. Like a – *(He punches the air.)* Like a punch thing.

LARRY. Yeah.

Yeah, okay.

CHET. Okay?

Okay. So. Annnnnd: *action*.

LARRY. At approximately 10:46 PM tonight, two young girls broke into Rick / Montgomery's trailer –

CHET. Yeah, like *(Does the punch.)*

*(**LARRY** forgets the karate chop. He stops.)*

LARRY. Shit.

CHET. It's okay it's okay keep going.

*(**LARRY** looks frustrated.)*

Hey come on. You got this man, you got it.

One more time. Come on.

You ready?

> (**LARRY** *nods.*)

Okay. Annnnnd: *action!*

LARRY. At approximately 10:46 AM tonight, two young women *(Air punches.)* broke in to Rick Montgomery's trailer. Right before he was about to give a highly enjoyable concert.

> (**CHET**'s *nodding and giving him the thumbs up from behind the camera.*)

A concert that was well-attended!

A concert that was family-friendly!

With lots of happy family members enjoying their evenings. Until, they were uuhhhhhh until they were… uhhhhh.

CHET. *(Trying to remember.)* Uh, untillllllll, uh…

LARRY. Shit!

CHET. Nah nah just improvise keep it going. Until they werrrrrrre caught off *guard*! By the likes of the… people! And –

LARRY. Just cut it Chet.

CHET. No come on man you can do it!

> (**LARRY** *folds his arms.*)

What's wrong?

LARRY. …Do I look stupid doing this?

CHET. Nah that – dude, you're *killin'* it.

The punch thing? You're killin' it dude.

LARRY. *(He looks down.)* Nahh I look stupid doing this.

CHET. No, come on man, you got it. You – no don't take off the hat.

(**LARRY** *takes off his hat.*)

Nooooo come on, what are you doin'?

LARRY. No one's gonna take this seriously.

CHET. Yes they will! You look like a total stud up there man, you look like you're in an action movie talkin' like that.

LARRY. *(Not convinced.)* Yeah...

CHET. Dude everyone's gonna see this and think you're totally awesome man.

This is gonna be the greatest YouTube series anyone's ever seen!

People are gonna fuckin' subscribe to this shit just to see *you*, man.

Officer McClasky.

In the field.

You know?

Bad guys beware!

This is totally gonna rehabilitate your image!

LARRY. You think so?

CHET. Totally! Everyone's gonna think of you as this action star man.

Not as the cop from that McDonald's thing.

LARRY. Mm.

CHET. And with these bodycams they got us? We're gonna be filming *all the time*.

It's gonna be sweet!

LARRY. ...You think Megan will watch it?

CHET. Hell yeah man! Megan's gonna see this and be like, "Who's that sweet-ass dad layin' down the law?"

Is that Bruce Willis up there? Is that Matthew McConaughey?

No man. That's *Larry*!

LARRY. I tell you she doesn't call me dad anymore? We're uh, officially on a first name basis.

CHET. That's just teenage chicks, man.

My niece? Dude. We used to go out behind my sister's house and blow shit up in the woods together *all the time*. It was awesome. And then she turned thirteen and all of a sudden it's like

That's not an okay thing to do anymore. You know?

LARRY. I can't even call her "Pickle" anymore.

CHET. Yeah well after this? You can call her whatever the fuck you want, man.

This is the crime of the century and you're the star of the show.

Everyone's gonna be talking about this!

LARRY. Yeah.

CHET. Talking about *you*.

LARRY. Maybe.

CHET. Come on, Megan's gonna think you're an all-American dad.

Your image is totally gonna be rehabilitated.

And I'm gonna get a buncha hits on my YouTube channel!

All you gotta do is dictate man.

Dictate the dictation. *"These girls SHALL NOT get away with this shit!"* – You know what I'm sayin', punch the words.

LARRY. Police aren't allowed to say shit on camera.

CHET. Nah nah nah it'll be totally cool. It's like a slip of the tongue, right?

Like you know you're not supposed to say it but you say it anyway, 'cause you're just so passionate about catchin' these chicks.

People are gonna see that and connect with it man.

Connect with *you*.

    (**LARRY** *considers it.*)

LARRY. ...Okay.

CHET. Okay?

LARRY. Yeah, okay.

CHET. Okay.

Hey: Bruce Willis, man.

    (**LARRY** *nods and puts his hat back on.*)

Aaaaaaaaaaand *action*.

LARRY. (*Like a fucking star.*) At approximately 10:46 in the PM tonight, two young teenage females broke into Rick Montgomery's trailer right before he was to give a highly enjoyable concert at the Cynthia Woods Mitchell Pavilion.

A concert that was well-attended.

That was family-friendly.

Until these young females broke into Rick's trailer and *kidnapped him*.

Witnesses say they saw the two girls fleeing the scene with Mr. Montgomery in a red 1993 Geo.

Rick Montgomery: if you are seeing this, we have a message for you:

WE WILL FIND YOU RICK.

CHET AND I WILL FIND YOU.

THESE GIRLS SHALL NOT GET AWAY WITH THIS SHIT!

    (Hard blackout.)

Scene Three

(Kimmy's bedroom.)

*(**MEGAN** is duct-taping a fifty-year-old unconscious **MAN** to Kimmy's My Little Pony desk chair. **KIMMY** is holding the unconscious **MAN** steady. They've put a bag or a shirt or something over his head. This **MAN**...is **RICK MONTGOMERY**.)*

KIMMY. Do you think maybe I should get him a Band-Aid?

MEGAN. Why?

KIMMY. I think you broke his nose.

MEGAN. Why would a Band-Aid fix a broken nose?

KIMMY. Or maybe an ice pack?

MEGAN. He's fine.

KIMMY. Why did you punch him so hard?

MEGAN. He surprised me.

KIMMY. ...It looks like you punched him a couple times though.

MEGAN. Whoa whoa, this is not *my* fault.

He wasn't even supposed to be done with his concert yet. I was supposed to have another hour in there.

If he hadn't have shown up and like, *interrupted* me.

And started shouting and causing a scene, I wouldn't have had to take him down.

KIMMY. Yeah but... *(Quietly.)* How come you pulled him into the car after you knocked him unconscious?

MEGAN. Because he saw me, Kimmy. He *saw* me.

We can't leave any witnesses.

KIMMY. I thought you had your mask on.

MEGAN. And anyway. *Anyway.* You were supposed to be looking out for me. How come you didn't see him?

KIMMY. I did but the horn in my grandma's car is broken.

MEGAN. Why didn't you yell or something?!

KIMMY. I don't know! I got scared…

(*Short pause.*)

…What are we gonna do with him?

MEGAN. Well.

The guitar wasn't in the trailer. So we gotta find out where it is.

KIMMY. How're we gonna do that?

MEGAN. (*Ominous.*) …I guess we're just gonna have to ask him.

KIMMY. You said that like you're not *just* gonna ask him.

(**MEGAN** *smiles at her.*)

(*Not liking this.*) Aw maaaaan.

MEGAN. It'll be fine.

KIMMY. We can't just let him go?

MEGAN. No. We came here to do a mission. We're gonna finish the mission.

Also we already tied him to the chair.

KIMMY. (*Just realizing.*) Oh my God!!

MEGAN. What!

KIMMY. He's gonna see my room.

MEGAN. What?

KIMMY. He's gonna see my room!

Rick Montgomery's gonna see my room!

MEGAN. So?

KIMMY. So I haven't cleaned in like six years!

MEGAN. Who cares?

KIMMY. What if he sees all my stuff? He's gonna see all my stuff!

What if he sees my *throat cream*? Megan!

(**KIMMY** *hides her throat cream.*)

MEGAN. What are you doing?

KIMMY. I think we should get him out of here.

MEGAN. Kimmy, what are / you worried –

KIMMY. It's just not a good idea and, and – why don't we just let him go?

MEGAN. Not yet. It'll –

KIMMY. Or what if we told my grandma!

MEGAN. No – stop telling your grandma things Kimmy, goddamn!

KIMMY. She's really good at ideas.

MEGAN. Twenty thousand dollars Kimmy!

Okay? That's what we're talking about here, that's what the guitar is worth.

Twenty. Thousand.

How many voice lessons do you think that's gonna get you?

KIMMY. ...Enough to fix my voice?

MEGAN. Maybe!

(Sincerely.) Maybe...

> *(Somewhere during this **RICK** has woken up. We see his hooded head start looking around. Neither girl notices.)*

So just – Look. Just follow my lead when he wakes up.

We gotta provide a united front against him.

And then I swear we'll let him go, okay?

We'll dump him under the highway or something.

I promise.

KIMMY. *(Hesitant.)* ...Okay.

MEGAN. Okay?

KIMMY. But...could we not drop him under the highway?

MEGAN. Where do you want to dump him?

KIMMY. Maybe we could do that thing where –

Remember when we found that bird with the broken wing in your backyard?

And we kept it in your basement?

And fed him Froot Loops and Snickers until he got better?

And then set him free in the woods and sang "On the Wings of Love" and watched him fly away?

Can we do something like that?

MEGAN. Of course.

KIMMY. Okay.

RICK. What?

> *(They see he's awake.)*

MEGAN. HOLY SHIT!!   **KIMMY.** OH MY GOSH!!

(They freak out and hide behind things.)

(Pause.)

RICK. *(Legitimately asking.)* Hello?

KIMMY. *(Whispering to* **MEGAN**.*)* What do we do?!

MEGAN. *(Whispering to* **KIMMY**.*)* Put your mask back on!

RICK. Who's that?

(They put their masks back on.)

MEGAN. *(Whispering to* **KIMMY**.*)* Ready?

*(***KIMMY*** nods, terrified.)*

*(***MEGAN*** and* ***KIMMY*** *march out. And pull* ***RICK***'s hood off. He is seriously groggy and out of it.)*

RICK. *(Eyes adjusting to the light.)* Whoa.

MEGAN. *(With authority.)* Hey.

RICK. What?

MEGAN. Is your name Rick Montgomery?

RICK. What?

MEGAN. *Is your name Rick Montgomery?*

RICK. Where am I?

MEGAN. You are at an undisclosed location.	**KIMMY.** You're in my bedroom – disclosed location...

*(***MEGAN*** puts her head in her hand. Goddamn it Kimmy.)*

*(***RICK*** finally notices his bandaged arms and legs.)*

RICK. Whoa.

Okay.

(Holding up his bound hands.) So what's goin' on here?

MEGAN. You have been kidnapped.

KIMMY. *(Quiet.)* Accidentally.

MEGAN. So don't even *think* about trying shit. Or what happened to your face will seem like Sunday school!

RICK. What happened to my face?

KIMMY. You mighta got punched… *(Looks at* **MEGAN.***)* A couple times.

*(***RICK*** reaches up and touches his face.)*

Does it hurt?

RICK. I can't really feel anything.

KIMMY. Wow. Really?

RICK. I'm on a lot of drugs right now.

KIMMY. Like Advil?

RICK. …Yeah.

MEGAN. Alright enough with this face shit. Nobody cares about your face.

RICK. *(Realizing.)* You're the one who was smashin' everything in my trailer.

MEGAN. That's right.

RICK. How old are y'all?

MEGAN. Old enough for shit to get real.

Now we have some questions we're gonna ask you.

KIMMY. Yeah.

MEGAN. And we *will* get the answers.

KIMMY. And then we'll let you go.

MEGAN. We *might* let you go.

KIMMY. You said we were gonna let him go after.

MEGAN. *(Whispering.)* He doesn't need to know that.

KIMMY. *(Whispering.)* What if he gets scared?

MEGAN. *(Whispering.)* That's what we want!

KIMMY. *(Whispering.)* ...Yeah...

MEGAN. *(Whispering.) Come on. United front!*

KIMMY. *(Whispering.)* Yeah I know –

MEGAN. *(Whispering.)* Come on!

KIMMY. I said I know!

(Weird pause.)

RICK. Aw man. I've been kidnapped by twelve-year-olds.

KIMMY. Nuh-uh! I'm thirteen and Megan's fourteen!

MEGAN. Don't use my name, Kimmy!

RICK. *(Groan of disappointment in himself.)* Ooohh Jesus. Come on Rick.

MEGAN. Alright check it out! This is how shit's gonna go.

You're tied to a chair. Nobody knows where you are. We control your life.

Okay?

That's the situation. We *own* you.

Now we have a couple questions that we need the answers to. And you're gonna give us those answers.

So. You can take this seriously?

Or you can *not* take this seriously.

And I *hope* you don't take it seriously...

Because if you don't? I'll get to turn you over to my associate here.

I busted her out of juvie just for this. She's *crazy*.

KIMMY. I am crazy.

MEGAN. *Yeah*. So get the fuck ready Rick. Your time has come.

(Blackout.)

Scene Four

*(The back room of the police station. **LARRY**'s pulling files. **CHET**'s working the ancient desktop computer. It's like 2 AM. Suddenly, **PATTY** enters, dressed half in PJs, half in police uniform. **PATTY** is the Chief of Police. She walks in with a good amount of swagger and authority. Like she owns the place. Because she does. So deal with it.)*

PATTY. Larry.

LARRY. Chief?

CHET. Hey Chief!

LARRY. What are you doin' here?

CHET. We thought you went home.

PATTY. Yeah so remember like four hours ago when I was leavin' the station and y'all were like, "Hey Patty."

And I was like, "What."

And y'all were like, "We caught this kidnapping case."

And I was like, "Who is it?"

And y'all were like, "Rick Montgomery."

And I was like, "Who the fuck is Rick Montgomery?"

And y'all were like, "The country music singer."

And I was like, "Who listens to country music?"

And y'all were like, "Can we be the lead on the case?"

And I was, "Fine, as long as y'all don't go into overtime?"

LARRY. Yeah?

PATTY. WELL I LIED.

We are going *deep* into overtime on this one.

We're going so deep into overtime that we won't even be able to see *regular* time anymore.

LARRY. What? Why?   **CHET**. Cool!

PATTY. So it's 1 AM and I'm sittin' there talkin' to my stupid-ass kids 'cause they need money again.

When my phone starts ringin'.

I'm like: *somebody's got a death wish.*

So I pick it up and boom. Guess who it is?

LARRY. I don't know.   **CHET**. Your ex-husband?

PATTY. The goddamn *Governor of Texas!*

LARRY. Wow.   **CHET**. WHOA. WHAT! WHAT!

PATTY. How did the Governor get my cell phone number?

Doesn't. Matter.

Because it's 1 AM and the Gov has decided to call me from his own patio in the capital of this great state.

Turns out the Governor *loves* Rick Montgomery.

Turns out he makes playlists and shit and gives them to people for Christmas.

Turns out Rick is going to be playing at an election rally in two days' time.

So the Gov is taking a *personal. Interest.* In this case.

You know what that means?

CHET. We're gonna get to meet the Governor?!

PATTY. Wrong!

It means Patty's gonna get to meet the Governor.

It means Patty's gonna get a picture of him pinnin' a medal to my chest.

PATTY. Then I'm gonna blow that shit up the size of a movie poster and mail it to my ex-husband with the words "Suck It, Jerry" watermarked into the background.

It means I have just upgraded this case from priority red to priority holy-shit-we-need-to-figure-this-shit-out-right-the-fuck-now.

LARRY. Yes / ma'am.

CHET. Yes ma'am.

PATTY. If this case hits the twenty-four-hour mark we're gonna have to push it state-wide and let everyone know we're a buncha dipshits can't keep the gate shut in our backyard.

We are officially four hours in gentlemen. So what do we got? What's the update?

LARRY. Uhhhhhh. Well.

Well we had that eyewitness thing. Right? Telling us about / the two –

PATTY. Yeah yeah the two girls, the red 1993 Geo. Got it. I'm talking about the *update*.

What's the update?

LARRY. Wellllllllll we tried finding evidence in the trailer, but everything was smashed all to little pieces, so it was sorta hard finding anything useful.

PATTY. Was there any blood or semen onsite?

LARRY. Oh! Yeah. Yeah there was definitely blood.

Um... I'm not sure about the other thing...

PATTY. Why didn't you use the mini crime lab we got?

LARRY. *(Looks at his shoes.)* Uh...

PATTY. *Why didn't y'all use the mini crime lab we got?*

CHET. We don't really have the mini crime lab anymore.

PATTY. What happened to it?

CHET. It was in the trunk of the police cruiser during Larry's uh

During the *incident* where that guy got off with our / cruiser –

PATTY. *(This again.)* Oh Jesus Christ.

LARRY. Sorry... I really thought that he was –

PATTY. *(Face-palming.)* I, I can't. I can't talk about this again.

LARRY. Yeah, sorry.

> *(Slight pause where **PATTY** is face-palming.)*

PATTY. No more fuck-ups. Y'all understand?

CHET. Yes / ma'am.

LARRY. Yes.

PATTY. We are the goddamn *police department*. You understand?

LARRY. Yes ma'am.   **CHET**. Yes ma'am.

PATTY. You're supposed to be the veteran of the department here, Larry.

LARRY. I know.

PATTY. At this point I should put Burkholder and Hernandez on the case. But I'm gonna keep you two on it.

CHET. Aww, thanks chief!

PATTY. I don't want to, I have to!

Burkholder's in Vegas this weekend and Hernandez is with her kids.

Which means y'all are my A-team. Time to act like it.

LARRY. Yes ma'am.   **CHET.** Absolutely.

PATTY. So...okay.

So we literally got a trailer of evidence sittin' out there that we can't use.

That's fine. I mean it's pretty fucked up. But...okay.

So what else do we got to go on?

CHET. Uh... I might've found something?

PATTY. *Chet* found something?!

CHET. Right?! So. So I was on the DMV's website and did a search for 1993 Geos registered to folks in the area. But none of 'em came up as red, right? So I called my boy Leroy at the Paint Depot and he sent me a list of all the Geo paint jobs they've done in the past and I finally got it down to three vehicles it could be. All in our area. Does that sound like something we could use?

PATTY. God*damn* boy. That is some police work right there!

CHET. Naaaahhh-you-don't-have-to-say-that.

PATTY. Print that shit out right now and let's hunt these people down.

CHET. Cool!

> *(He presses print on the ancient desktop and the ancient printer burps to life.)*
>
> *(It's printing. It's printing. It's printing. It's printing. It takes basically forever for this thing to print. Seriously.)*
>
> *(Like, think five minutes. And then add some more time to that.)*
>
> *(It's ridiculous. It's printing. It's still printing. Aaaaand it finishes.)*

CHET. It printed! Yes!

PATTY. Alright. Let's split this up. I'm gonna drink a gallon of coffee and get on dispatch. Chet, bring around the cruiser. Let's go people!

> *(They run out of the room.* **LARRY** *stays standing there. One of the addresses has piqued his interest...)*

Scene Five

(Kimmy's room. **MEGAN** *and* **KIMMY** *are still wearing their masks. The interrogation is about to commence.)*

MEGAN. Okay here's how this is gonna go.

I'm gonna ask you a question. And every time you don't answer my friend here is gonna crush one of your fingers with a hammer, okay?

*(**RICK** looks at **KIMMY**. She gives a little wave.)*

RICK. Okay.

MEGAN. And if you lie or joke around, same consequence.

RICK. *(Still bored.)* Yep. Got it.

MEGAN. You think we're joking?! We are dead serious.

RICK. Look, just – tell me what y'all want. I'll give it to you, probably.

I don't have any money. If that's what y'all are after.

Or drugs. Everyone keeps taking 'em from me.

Assholes.

So just tell me, so we can all get outta here.

MEGAN. We want your 19. 27. Martin 45.

RICK. *That's* all? *That's* why y'all kidnapped me?

For a goddamn *guitar*?

MEGAN. Where is it?

RICK. Aw man. I feel like y'all made a mistake.

MEGAN. Is that you not answering a question?

RICK. I don't have it.

KIMMY. Oh!

Well that's okay then. Don't worry about it.

MEGAN. I don't believe you.

RICK. Why do you want my wife's guitar?

MEGAN. Um. DUH. It has a market price of like $20,000?

RICK. *(Laughs.)* Who told you that?

MEGAN. Amazon.

RICK. Yeah. Mint condition, maybe.

But you ever seen Mary's guitar?

It's been busted, broken, chipped, restrung, broken again – it even got burned one time, which was weird.

It's only good for sentimental value…and she wasn't very sentimental towards me at the end.

So I don't have it.

KIMMY. I was really sorry to hear of her passing…

RICK. Yeah.

Well.

…Thanks.

KIMMY. Cancer's terrible.

My parents died too.

Not from cancer but from getting drunk one night and driving into the side of a Walmart.

My grandma said it's sorta the same thing though.

RICK. Okay.

MEGAN. What's sentimental about it?

(**RICK** *looks at her.*)

You said the guitar's sentimental.

RICK. Yeah. It was.

MEGAN. And?

RICK. Who are you?

MEGAN. Answer the question.

RICK. You first.

MEGAN. You wanna get some broken fingers bro?

RICK. Who are y'all?

And why am I in a child's bedroom?

KIMMY. It's because of her mom.

*(They both look at **KIMMY**.)*

Or – sorry.

But that's why, right?

She got it from her mom?

MEGAN. *(Whispering.) Kimmy!*

KIMMY. I'm sorry! But – it was in *Country Weekly*.

They had a whole feature on her.

*(To **RICK**.)* It was *really* good.

And like – yeah. She got the guitar from her mom.

And her mom got it from her grandma. And her grandma got it from a dumpster.

'Cause no one wanted it.

'Cause it was broken.

So she brought it home 'cause her daughter was a baby and crying and she didn't have things to calm her down like the internet or the Disney Channel.

So she took home the instrument.

And when she played it for her daughter, it didn't play perfect...but it played.

And even though her daughter didn't love it...she stopped being loud.

And it got passed down from mother to child ever since.

And that's why she loves it so much.

That's why she hasn't fixed it.

She wants it to sound the way it's always sounded. A little bit broken? A little bit off? But just right.

(Slight pause.)

Is what it said in *Country Weekly*... I'm a subscriber.

*(**RICK** has been quietly laughing near the end of this story.)*

What?

RICK. No, just...you know none of that's true, right?

KIMMY. *Country Weekly lied?*

RICK. Not exactly. See, Mary was uh...

(Smiling.) She liked to mess with people just to mess with people sometimes.

She kept getting questions about why she'd play this broken, old-ass guitar all the time.

And she couldn't tell the truth, so she made the whole thing up.

KIMMY. So...none of that's true?

RICK. I mean, I don't know.

It did belong to her mom. And her grandma before that. So it is kind of a family thing.

RICK. But the rest of it. (*Shakes his head.*)

She actually had to steal the damn thing from her mom. She wasn't going to let her have it.

Evil woman.

KIMMY. (*Suddenly excited.*) So how'd it actually get like that?

> (*Slight pause.* **RICK** *looks at them. Stops himself.*)

RICK. Ah. Nooo, that's okay.

KIMMY. Aw, come on, please?

We won't tell anyone.

RICK. Nah, it's not interesting.

MEGAN. Answer her question.

> (**RICK** *looks at* **MEGAN.** *Pause.*)

RICK. I was in Lubbock for a couple days for this festival.

> (**KIMMY** *sits down cross legged next to him, like it's story time.*)

And you know, it's Lubbock. So. Everything sucks basically.

And I'm thinkin' I'll probably ditch out early. Head to Austin. Dallas. Somewhere.

And I'm walkin' to my car when I hear this...woman.

Singin' this song like

She's callin' out to you.

Singing so soft, you can see the words rolling in the air towards you.

And if you don't pay attention, the words might not reach your ears.

So I make my way up front.

And there she is.

This tiny little thing. Surrounded by people…

And everyone's looking at her.

And she's lookin' back.

But she's only looking at one person.

KIMMY. *(Whispered.)* Was it you?

RICK. No it was not.

She was making eyes at this other guy up front.

And he was making the same kind of eyes back.

She's singing this farewell song to him. Like she's going somewhere.

And she finishes her song and people clap.

And they still haven't broken eye contact.

And she walks backstage. And he walks backstage. Still haven't broken eye contact.

And I'm looking at the way they're staring at each other.

And I'm thinking. If there's something like love out there, this is probably the closest I'll ever come to it.

This, right here.

These two people.

Just staring so hard that there's nothing else in the – BAM!

She hits him *directly* in the spine with her guitar.

I'm talking one shot! And he goes *dooown* like a dead body.

And that's when she *really* lays into him.

RICK. Bam. Bam. Bam.

Just like, *assaulting* this man. You know what I mean?

Like, prison-worthy assault.

Turns out this guy is her fiancé.

Who she just found out had been…not exactly true to her.

And he had apologized and they had made up.

But…she changed her mind.

So she sang him a goodbye song. And then *really* said goodbye.

And I'm starin' at her. Transfixed. Absolutely destroying this guy.

And she stopped and stared back at me.

And she said, "What! You wanna be next?"

And I was like,

"Yes ma'am I wanna be next."

Unfortunately she had to run 'cause the guy was starting to bleed on the ground.

I found her a couple days later trying to get someone to fix her 45 she had just caved in on this guy's back.

So I reset the strings.

Fixed the neck.

But she wanted to keep the caved in parts caved in.

She wanted to keep it as a reminder.

Not to let transgressions go unpunished.

And I was like…Jesus. This woman.

This woman is fire itself.

This woman is the kind of fire you need for the winter.

The kind of fire you need to illuminate things.

The kind of fire you need to survive.

KIMMY. *(Whispered.)* Wow.

I wanna survive with fire.

RICK. No. You don't.

KIMMY. What? Why?

RICK. 'Cause no matter what.

You're not gonna be ready for when it goes out.

Especially when you're not seeing eye to eye on things.

KIMMY. *(Heartbroken.)* Oh my God.

MEGAN. *(Dry.)* Yeah. Heartbreaking. I still don't believe you though. I don't believe you don't know where it is.

RICK. I don't.

MEGAN. That fucking long ass story, are you kidding me?! That's bullshit.

You *absolutely* know.

RICK. Even if I did, I wouldn't tell you.

MEGAN. Do I have to go over the consequences of what happens when you don't answer questions again?

RICK. Bring it on dude. Go ahead and smash alllll these guys.

MEGAN. That can be arranged!

RICK. Great! Have yourself a day!

MEGAN. We will!

(To **KIMMY.***)* Okay. Give it to him.

KIMMY. ...What?

MEGAN. Give it to him!

KIMMY. But... *(Quiet.)* I don't wanna give it to him.

> (**MEGAN** *grabs the hammer.*)

MEGAN. I'm gonna give you until three, and then I'm breakin' shit.

RICK. Here, I'll lay 'em out for you. How's that?

MEGAN. You think I won't?

RICK. Nah I'm sure you'll be great. Go for it.

MEGAN. I'm counting to three! One.

RICK. Just do it.

MEGAN. I will.

RICK. Two!

MEGAN. Two!

Stop counting for me!

RICK. Three!

> *(She swings the hammer back. And the doorbell rings... Everything stops for a second.)*

MEGAN. *(Loud whispering.)* Who is that?

KIMMY. *(Loud whispering.)* I don't know. Nobody ever visits us.

> *(The doorbell rings again. **MEGAN** goes to the window and looks out [discreetly]. **KIMMY** follows suit.)*

MEGAN. Oh my God.

KIMMY. Why is your dad here?

MEGAN. *(To herself.)* God damn it Larry.

...Okay. You stay here. I'll take care of this.

If he tries anything...

*(She hands **KIMMY** the hammer.).*

*(**MEGAN** leaves.)*

RICK. You got one crazy friend right there.

KIMMY. She means really well.

RICK. She calls her dad Larry.

KIMMY. What?

RICK. You don't mean well when you call your parents by their first names.

KIMMY. Well. Technically he's her adopted dad? So she said it technically doesn't count.

RICK. Adopted dad...

KIMMY. It's when you're born without any parents, and / then –

RICK. I know what it is.

...What're you getting out of all this?

KIMMY. *(Duh.)* Ummmm. I feel like we just spent a lot of time talking about that? / So I'm –

RICK. No, that's her. I'm talking about *you*. What are *you* doing here?

You don't seem like the kidnappin' type.

KIMMY. Oh! Well. Like a week ago? Megan came up to me at school? And was like

"Hey! Did you hear about the Rick Montgomery concert?"

I was like, "*Yes.* 'Cause he's the best." ('Cause *(Quiet.)* you are.)

KIMMY. And she was like, "Great! We're gonna break into his place and rob him!"

And I was like, "Whhhh– nooo that doesn't sound like a good idea."

And she was like, "But it'll be so much fun!"

And I was like, "What if we just broke into the concert and had so much fun listening to the melodies?"

And then she got real silent? And sad? And didn't talk to me for six hours?

And it made my heart feel like a big cavern.

So I agreed to do it.

RICK. Ahh. You got manipulated.

KIMMY. Nuh-uh.

RICK. Yeah.

KIMMY. Well – but I couldn't let her go alone! What if something happened to her? She's my soul friend.

RICK. ...She's what?

KIMMY. You know how sometimes you meet someone who's like, feels like you've known them since before you were born?

Like since you were both just a couple of souls hanging out in Heaven together waiting to get born?

That's what she is. My soul friend.

RICK. You shouldn't let people tell you what to do.

KIMMY. She wasn't telling me what to do she's my soul friend! Haven't you ever had a soul friend?

(Brief pause.)

RICK. Yeah.

KIMMY. *(Understanding.)* Yeah.

And didn't you do everything your soul friend said?

RICK. ...Yeah.

KIMMY. And didn't it break your heart into a million aches when they stopped talking to you for six hours?

RICK. Yeah.

KIMMY. Yeah.

> *(He doesn't respond.)*

Hey. Have you ever thought of having like a protégé?

RICK. No.

KIMMY. 'Cause I don't know if you've heard of the show *The Voice*? / But –

RICK. No.

KIMMY. Okay but what if like someone was to audition for you and they were really great?

> *(Pause. **RICK** considers.)*

RICK. Tell you what. You do me a favor, I'll do you a favor.

KIMMY. Really??

RICK. See my boot?

In the bottom there's a little bag of white pills.

KIMMY. Why is it in your boot?

RICK. 'Cause I'm hiding them, duh.

Now I need you to reach down deep and grab 'em.

> *(She moves towards him, a little disgusted at this.)*

You'll probably have to cut the duct tape first.

KIMMY. Oh…

RICK. What.

KIMMY. I don't think I can do that.

I don't think Megan would like that.

RICK. You remember what I said about people tellin' you what to do?

KIMMY. …Yeah?

RICK. 'Cause here's the thing. If you undo the tape? I'll let you sing a song.

>   (**KIMMY** *goes stone-faced.*)

KIMMY. *(Dropping a couple octaves.)* What?

RICK. What?

KIMMY. *(Heavy whisper.)* Are you serious?

RICK. Yeah. One song.

KIMMY. *(Heavy whisper.)* Oh my God.

RICK. Is that a yes?

>   (**KIMMY** *opens her mouth and lets out the loudest squeal of joy, shock, nervousness, and delight the world has ever known. Blackout.*)

Scene Six

(Kimmy's driveway. **MEGAN** *opens the front door and steps outside.* **CHET**'s *holding his bodycam like it's a movie camera.)*

MEGAN. Why are you here?

LARRY. *(Surprised to see her.)* Heeey sweetheart.

MEGAN. Hi.

What are you doing here?

LARRY. Oh, well we were just – Chet and I were just comin' by to check something out with Mrs. Womack.

MEGAN. Why does Chet have a camera?

CHET. We're makin' a YouTube series!

MEGAN. ...What.

LARRY. It's / nothing.

CHET. Okay. Okay. You ever hear of *Cops*? Well this is like *Cops*, but better.

We're callin' it "Cops!" Subtitle: *(In a cool voice.)* "of Sheepshead County."

And your dad's the star!

MEGAN. He's not my dad.

CHET. Well...he's still the star!

LARRY. We're not actually – it's not a real YouTube thing.

CHET. What hell yeah it is. This is going up on my Channel. Chet-the-Star-King-800. I have subscribers.

We're filming at this very moment!

MEGAN. I'm being filmed?!

LARRY. No, no, we're – no. Chet.

CHET. We're gettin' so much good footage here though.

LARRY. *Chet.* Just – come on. Alright?

>   (**CHET** *turns off the camera. Sulks.*)

Sorry hon'.

MEGAN. Please don't call me that.

LARRY. So uh…did you spend the night over here, or…?

MEGAN. Yes.

LARRY. *(Confused.)* Oh.

MEGAN. I told you about this. I told you this was happening. Stop pretending you / don't know.

LARRY. No, it's not that –

MEGAN. You can't keep showing up at my friends' houses like this. Pretending you don't know I'm here?

Like you have "cop stuff" to check up on?

LARRY. No I know. / Just –

MEGAN. It's weird. My friends think you're weird.

>   (*Short pause.*)

LARRY. *(Sorta quiet.)* I just like makin' sure you're okay, is all.

CHET. Yeah he just likes checkin' up on you.

LARRY. Just wanna know where you are. Sorry if that's… you know.

MEGAN. Okay well stop. It's weird. You can just call.

LARRY. Yeah. Okay… Sorry…

CHET. *(To no one…)* Probably wouldn't need to show up if you actually *(Mumbling?)* picked up the phone though.

LARRY. *(Whispered to* **CHET.***)* Chet.

CHET. Just sayin' man.

LARRY. *(Whispered to CHET.)* Okay, well, it's fine.

CHET. *(Whispered to LARRY.)* I know it is, I'm just sayin', you know.

LARRY. *(Whispered to CHET.)* Okay.

CHET. *(Whispered to LARRY.)* You always get upset when she doesn't / pick up –

LARRY. *(Whispered to CHET.)* I do not get upset.

CHET. *(Whispered to LARRY.)* Yeah you do dude, you get / *so* upset –

LARRY. *(Loud whispering to CHET.)* It's fine Chet it's fine.

CHET. *(Loud whispering to LARRY.)* I'm just sayin' dude! You know?

LARRY. Okay Chet.

CHET. Hey man, I'm just doin' this for you. You know?

LARRY. *(Louder.)* Okay Chet.

CHET. I'm out here for you, man.

LARRY. *(Louder still.)* Okay Chet thank you that's fine thank you!

(Weird pause.)

MEGAN. Okay. Well... Bye.

(She tries to go back inside.)

LARRY. Whoa whoa hey. Uh. Actually – sorry. We actually do have cop stuff to check up on.

Gotta talk to her about her car.

MEGAN. ...What about her car?

LARRY. Just got a couple questions.

MEGAN. Weeeeeeeell you can't talk to her right now. Because she's...sleeping.

LARRY. Really? We just talked to her.

(*To* **CHET.**) Right?

CHET. Yeah just talked to her, said we were comin' over. She was like, "sweet."

LARRY. (*Reassuring.*) We won't bother y'all. Whatever you and Kimberly are doing. I won't even say hi if you don't want.

(*They walk to the door.*)

MEGAN. Wait you can't!

LARRY. Wh– why not?

MEGAN. Just...because.

LARRY. Well...we kinda have to talk to her.

CHET. It's a time sensitive thing.

LARRY. It's just a coupla questions. We'll be gone so soon you won't even know.

(*They go for the door again.*)

MEGAN. (*Blurting out.*) *Wait* okay I lied to you!

(*They stop. Short pause.*)

You were right. I didn't tell you I was staying at Kimmy's tonight. I lied to you.

And...I didn't tell you about it...on purpose.

LARRY. ...Why?

MEGAN. Because I didn't want you to know about your... surprise...birthday present!

LARRY. (*Like, really touched.*) You got me a birthday present?

MEGAN. 'Cause your birthday's coming up, right? Aprilllllllll 11th?

LARRY. Yeah, April 11th!

CHET. Isn't it the 15th?

MEGAN. That's why I came over last night and couldn't tell you.

Kimmy and her grandma have been helping me make it. We've been up all night.

LARRY. Awww you didn't have to do that...

CHET. What is it?

MEGAN. It's a surprise. And if you go in there, you're gonna spoil it.

You don't want to spoil your surprise, right?

LARRY. No I don't wanna spoil my surprise.

MEGAN. Exactly. 'Cause that would be rude. And then it wouldn't be a surprise.

LARRY. *(To* **CHET.***)* She's right, it wouldn't be a surprise anymore.

MEGAN. Okay. So...y'all can come back later then.

CHET. Yeah or we could just talk to her out here on the porch.

(Beat. **CHET** *goes to ring the doorbell.)*

MEGAN. Wait-you-can't-do-that-either!

(She blocks them.)

Look. You know how Kimmy's grandma is. She's such a chatter mouth. She can't keep any secrets to herself anymore. And I really don't want it ruined because it's special and I've been working on it all night and I think if you talk to her she'll ruin it even though she won't mean to ruin it you know what I mean?

LARRY. You think so?

MEGAN. I *totally* think so. I mean, what do you have to talk to Kimmy's grandma about anyway?

It's not like me or Kimmy or her grandma or her car left the house at all last night.

LARRY. Well.

MEGAN. I mean, what? You don't think Kimmy's grandma is some kind of criminal, right?

> *(She starts laughing. Like she and **LARRY** are joking around.)*

LARRY. Yeah. Ha.

MEGAN. *(Starts laughing.)* I mean that would be crazy...

LARRY. *(Smiling.)* Yeah. Yeah that would be like.

Like if that was a movie that would be like. Like: "Grandma Gone Wild" or something.

MEGAN. *(Laughs harder.)* Yeah.

LARRY. Or no like, like: "Grandma Gone," you know... *(Thinking.)* ..."*Crazy!*" or something.

MEGAN. *(Playfully pushes him.)* That's funny. You're so funny!

LARRY. *(Embarrassed.)* Naaahhhhhjjmmm.

CHET. Yeah or like, "Grandma's Fucked Up Day Out!"

> *(Nobody laughs. Weird pause.)*

Or...

LARRY. Hey! You know. Maybe, uh. If you weren't like. Like if you're not doin' anything later tonight. Um. For dinner.

I was thinkin' of maybe makin' some Fish Tacos.

MEGAN. *(His food is terrible.)* Coooooolll yyeaaahhh.

LARRY. Yeah? 'Cause you know your mom's not in town this weekend, so I was thinking, you know. It could be pretty. Pretty cool. Fish Tacos and then. And then maybe we could watch like *Deep Impact* afterwards?!

MEGAN. Definitely. That's definitely a possibility.

LARRY. Dinner and movie night!

MEGAN. Yeah. I'll think about it.

LARRY. Alright. Alright. Well...*cool.*

MEGAN. Cool... *(Pause.) Anyway.* I'm gonna go back inside now. To continue with the, your, thing.

LARRY. Okay. Yeah.

Don't tell me what it is.

MEGAN. Oh I won't.

LARRY. Okay. Ha.

MEGAN. And y'all are gonna go now. Right...*Dad*?

LARRY. *(Total elation.)* Yeah-yeah-right-sure-I-mean-whatever-you-yeah.

MEGAN. Good... See you tonight.

> (**LARRY** *opens his arms for a hug.* **MEGAN** *hesitates. Then slowly, ever so slowly, walks in for the hug. Then turns and runs inside.)*

LARRY. I'll see you / tonight!

> *(She's already closed the door. There's a moment. Then:)*

CHET. DUDE! Did you see that?! Dude that was *amazing*.

> (**LARRY**'s *getting really emotional, but he doesn't want to show it.)*

CHET. See what I'm sayin' man?! *Connection.*

She saw you reachin' out and she reached right back!

That was like badass TV movie magic, man!

LARRY. WE DID IT!

CHET. What?

LARRY. WE DID IT!!

CHET. Yeah! That's right man. *You* did it!

LARRY. Excellent job Officer Walker!

CHET. Excellent job Officer McClasky!

(**LARRY** *salutes him for some reason. Blackout.*)

Scene Seven

(Kimmy's bedroom. **KIMMY** *has her guitar strapped on. She's not wearing her mask anymore because this is her star moment and stars don't wear masks.* **RICK** *has been situated so that his chair is a sort of "audience" for what's about to happen.)*

KIMMY. Okay.

So.

This is a song I wrote?

It's called "Star Quality."

It's about love.

And perseverance.

And the time I got voted out of the school choir by my friends.

And I've never sung it for anyone in my whole life.

(She takes a deep breath.)

Okay.

(She turns around so her back is to him.)

(Gets into a stance.)

(Takes a moment. Then:)

(She starts playing. The music comes in short staccato bursts, punctuated by a pause in which **KIMMY** *turns her head to give* **RICK** *a coy look.)*

(Yeah. This is a routine she has practiced.)

(More than a couple of times.)

KIMMY.
>THEY
>SAID TO ME
>HEY KIM-MY
>YOU SUCK I HATE YOU.
>
>YOU
>SOUND JUST LIKE
>YOUR WINDPIPE
>GOT CRUSHED IN PRE-SCHOOL.
>
>WHAT THEY CAN'T SEE
>ARE THE FACTS INSIDE OF ME.
>ONE AND ONE MAKE TWO
>AND TWO AND ONE MAKE THREE
>
>I THINK THIS MIGHT BE
>THE TIME FOR IT TO BREAK FREE
>BREAK FREE
>
>I'VE GOT STAAAAAAR QUALITYYYYYY
>JUST BETWEEN YOU-U AND ME
>STAAAAAAR QUALITYYYYYY
>AND THE WORLD WILL SEE
>
>WHEN I STEP OUT
>AND OPEN MY MOUTH
>EV'RYONE WILL SHOUT
>YOU'VE GOT STAAAAAAR QUALITYYYYYY
>AND I HOPE YOU WILL A-GREE
>
>>*(Short instrumental.* **KIMMY**'s *getting into it. She does a wild left kick for punctuation.)*
>
>I
>CRIED ALONE
>ON THE PHONE
>TO MY GRANDMA
>
>SHE
>SAID TO ME

DON'T WORRY
LIKE THEY DON'T HAVE FLAWS

THEY DON'T SEE
EV'RYTHING I SEE IN YOU.
I ALSO PRAYED TO GOD, HE SAID
THAT HE NOTICED TOO.

HE TOLD ME YOU'LL BE
YOU'LL BE
YOU'LL BE

A PERSON WITH STAAAAAR QUALITYYYYYYY
JUST BETWEEN YOU-U AND ME
STAAAAAAR QUALITYYYYYY
AND THE WORLD WILL SEE

WHEN YOU STEP OUT
AND OPEN YOUR MOUTH
EV'RYONE WILL SHOUT
YOU'VE GOT STAAAAAAR QUALITYYYYYY
AND I KNOW YOU WILL A-GREE

> (**KIMMY** *jumps onto her bed and goes into a full on bridge. She's rocking out. She can actually play the guitar really well. She's doing some kind of weird, physical dance thing while playing on her bed. She suddenly stops and goes a cappella.*)

'CAUSE THEY DON'T UNDERSTAND ALL THE FACTS INSIDE OF ME
ONE AND ONE MAKE TWO AND TWO AND ONE MAKE THREE
YOU JUST GOTTA FOLLOW YOUR DREAMS
AND YOUR *(Mumbles/hasn't written these lyrics.)* SSCCHHEEMMMEEEEEEESSS.

I'VE GOT STAAAAAAR QUALITYYYYYY
JUST BETWEEN YOU-U AND ME
STAAAAAAR QUALITYYYYYY
AND THE WORLD WILL SEE

KIMMY.
>WHEN I STEP OUT
>AND OPEN MY MOUTH
>EV'RYONE WILL SHOUT
>THAT I'VE GOT STAAAAAAR QUALITYYYYYY
>AND I HOPE YOU WILL AGREE

>*(She nails the last chord. And stands there, totally winded and emotionally drained.)*

>*(This is probably the most triumphant, vulnerable moment in **KIMMY**'s short life. After catching her breath, she composes herself.)*

So...what's up? What do you think?

RICK. Well goddamn.

That was a goddamn performance is what that was.

KIMMY. *(Blushing.)* Nooo, you're lying, shut up, okay.

RICK. Woo! The energy? The enthusiasm?

The weird, whatever that was on the bed?

KIMMY. *(Blushing more.)* No stop what else?

RICK. You play a mean-ass guitar, you know that? Where'd you learn that?

KIMMY. My grandma taught me?

RICK. Go grandma.

KIMMY. Does that mean...does that you mean you might wanna...mentor me?

RICK. What was that thing I heard in your voice?

KIMMY. What do you mean?

RICK. There was something in your voice...

It sounded like uh, like you've got uh...

KIMMY. *(Heavy-whisper.)* star quality?

RICK. No. Vocal scarring. That's what it is.

KIMMY. *(Quieter.)* I thought maybe you wouldn't notice…

RICK. What happened to it?

KIMMY. Well. Remember when, in my song I talked about the kids making fun of me and thinking my windpipe got crushed in pre-school? Well my windpipe sort of did get a little bit crushed in pre-school. 'Cause I was accidentally in the backseat when my parents accidentally drove into the side of that Walmart? And I had to have to have a surgery on my vocal cords after? And the doctors said I suffered from something called "blunt force trauma"? But it's okay! 'Cause my voice teacher Ms. Cafeo? Said that if you just practice a lot, then it could heal naturally all by itself! So she's having me take a lot of extra lessons.

RICK. Yeah. Well. Ms. Cafeo is a little bit of a liar.

KIMMY. …What?

RICK. Your vocal fold is made to be all loose wiggly. So it can vibrate as it wants. The scarring takes that whole thing and stiffens it up. Like a fist. And once scarred… can't get un-scarred..

KIMMY. But…nuh-uh.

RICK. Sorry.

KIMMY. I think, I think you're thinking of a different vocal scarring. I have the kind that gets better after you take a bunch of voice lessons.

RICK. Only one kind.

KIMMY. No, 'cause Ms. Cafeo said that if I just practice a whole lot that – What if I practice more? What if I just practice a whole lot more?! That's what I should do, right?!

RICK. Honestly?

KIMMY. Yes, honestly?!

RICK. Honestly you should probably quit.

KIMMY. *Singing?*

RICK. While you're young. It'll save you a lot of time. And pain.

KIMMY. But...but you said I was really good. You said "that" was a performance.

RICK. And it was. You're a goddamn performer. You can light up a room as bright as a collapsing fucking star.

...But you're never gonna sing. That's just a fact.

KIMMY. Oh my god.

(She collapses like a wet paper bag, heartbroken.)

What am I supposed to do with the rest of my life?

RICK. Well. You can sure as shit play the shit out of that guitar.

KIMMY. *(Like a lost puppy.)* I'm not supposed to just play the guitar...

RICK. Yeah well we don't always get what we want.

(Pause.)

But deal's a deal though, right?

KIMMY. What?

RICK. Our deal.

(He indicates his boot.)

KIMMY. ...I don't know if that's a good idea anymore.

RICK. What.

KIMMY. I don't think I'm gonna do that.

RICK. You can't back out on a deal.

That's why people make deals, 'cause you can't back out on 'em.

KIMMY. No, Megan was right, you're a liar.

RICK. Deal's a deal!

KIMMY. No, you're a liar! And I'm gonna tell everyone you're a liar! And then I'm gonna sing all the songs in the world! And I'm gonna have a great career! And I'm not gonna give you this picture I painted of you either!

(**MEGAN** *busts back in.*)

MEGAN. *(Harsh whisper.)* Shut up. Shut up. Everyone can hear y'all. What are you doing on the bed?!

KIMMY. Mr. Montgomery's being a *jerk*!

MEGAN. Where's your mask?!

KIMMY. My what?!

MEGAN. Your *mask* Kimmy!

KIMMY. Aw crap, I think I lost it when I sang my song.

MEGAN. When *what*?

KIMMY. Where's yours?

(**MEGAN** *checks and, yep. She forgot to put hers back on after being outside.*)

RICK. *You.* That's where I know you from.

KIMMY. What?

RICK. You're that fan.

MEGAN. What are you talking about?

RICK. You've been to our shows.

You've been backstage.

You've talked to my wife!

KIMMY. What?

MEGAN. He doesn't know what he's saying, he's drugged up.

RICK. Like five times you've been to our shows. I fuckin' know you.

MEGAN. Alright enough of this bullshit, we're out of time.

Just tell me where it is and we'll let you go. Okay?

RICK. No, now I wanna know why.

MEGAN. This is your last warning dude!!

RICK. Come here…look at me.

MEGAN. Where is it?

RICK. Why do you want that thing so bad?

MEGAN. For the money dipshit!

RICK. Nope. Try again.

MEGAN. That's all!

RICK. Tell me the truth.

MEGAN. And also…it belongs to me.

RICK. What?

MEGAN. It belongs to me.

(He looks at her. And figures it out.)

RICK. Awwww shit.

Are you serious?

KIMMY. …What?

RICK. Ooohhh man.

I did *not* think I'd be figurin' this shit out *this* way.

Wow.

Okay.

KIMMY. Figure what out?

What's he talking about?

RICK. She doesn't know?

KIMMY. I don't know what?

RICK. You didn't tell your friend?

MEGAN. *(To* **RICK.***)* Don't.

KIMMY. Tell me what?

RICK. I thought y'all were soul sisters, or, / whatever –

KIMMY. Soul friends! What are you talking about?

What's he talking about?

RICK. Your friend here. She's –

> *(***MEGAN** *abruptly smashes his fingers with the hammer.)*

KIMMY. OH MY GOD!   **RICK.** OOOOHHHHH!!!!!

MEGAN. *(Even she's surprised.)* Whoa!

RICK. Fuckin' broke my fuckin' fingers!

MEGAN. That's right I'll do it again, too!

KIMMY. Megan!!

RICK. Goddamn it, give me that!

> *(***RICK** *grabs the hammer out of her hands.)*

MEGAN. Hey!

RICK. *(Holding it out defensively.)* Whoooaaaa back up!

MEGAN. Give it back!

RICK. Let's everybody just back up now!

> (**MEGAN** *grabs a little statue of a cow or something from Kimmy's desk and wields it like a weapon.*)

MEGAN. Give it back! I'm not even joking!

RICK. No!

No more of this Rick getting punched and hit with a hammer and all this other shit.

Alright?

We're all just gonna take a second and chill the fuck out.

Put down the cow.

...Put down the cow.

Okay don't put down the cow.

But here's how this is gonna go.

Now I could probably escape outta here with this thing if I really wanted to.

Probably.

Maybe not.

I don't know.

Point is, I'm not going to.

You got me?

Instead. I'll make you a deal.

MEGAN. ...What deal?

RICK. You want that guitar so bad? It belongs to you?

Okay.

You untie me? And I'll take you to it.

MEGAN. ...Give me back the hammer first.

RICK. Is it a deal?

MEGAN. Where is it?

RICK. We got a house.

A couple hours down I-10. In La Grange.

You untie me, I'll drive you there and drive you back.

> *(She looks uncertain.* **RICK** *extends the hammer out to her, handle first. She grabs it.)*

MEGAN. Deal.

KIMMY. Megan!

MEGAN. But if you try anything. I swear to God.

KIMMY. What are you doing?!

MEGAN. Don't worry, it'll be fine.

KIMMY. But I don't even know what's going on. What's going on right now?

MEGAN. I'll, explain later.

KIMMY. I don't think you should go. *(Loud whisper.)* He's not trustworthy.

MEGAN. Look, it's *fine*. Just cut him loose, okay?

KIMMY. No. That's not – that wasn't a, a suggestion. I'm telling you.

I don't want you to go.

MEGAN. Kimmy...

KIMMY. No! You always say that!

You always say "Kimmy" like in a really soft and nurturing tone so I'll do whatever you want, but not this time!

KIMMY. This is my bedroom and in my bedroom what I say goes because I am, the...*queen*...of, the bedroom.

So.

And that's what I'm saying!

You can't go with him.

>   (*Pause.*)

Please.

>   (**MEGAN** *grabs a pair of scissors from the desk and cuts* **RICK** *loose.*)

MEGAN. I'll be back soon. Okay?

KIMMY. ...Can I at least go with you?

MEGAN. Not this time.

KIMMY. But...we're not supposed to separate. Remember?

We can't be "Megimmy" if we're not together.

Then I'd just be Kimmy...and I hate being Kimmy.

MEGAN. I'll be right back.

>   (**MEGAN** *and* **RICK** *leave.*)
>
>   (**KIMMY***'s left alone in her room.*)
>
>   (*Blackout.*)

Scene Eight

(The police station. **PATTY** *is reaming out* **CHET** *and* **LARRY**.*)*

PATTY. Nothin'? Y'all got nothin'?

Not even a *suspect*?!

LARRY. Well Patty, that's not exactly –

PATTY. Ah, that wasn't a question, that was a statement with a question mark at the end.

I *know* you don't have a suspect because when y'all came in you weren't talking about "let's look up this guy's records" or "let's hunt down this guy's family members" you were talkin' about fuckin' fish fuckin' tacos!

CHET. Sorry. **LARRY**. …Sorry.

PATTY. Do you know who just called again from the state capital?

CHET. *(Really excited.)* The Governor?!

PATTY. Wrong!

The Governor's Chief of Staff.

CHET. *(Sotto.)* Whoa.

PATTY. He was like, "When am I gonna get my FUCKIN' updates Patricia?"

I was like, "You give me thirty minutes, Gary. And I will give you your updates."

He said, "Good. 'Cause I got a timer here on my desk. I'm pressing the start button right now."

I said, "Sweet baby doll, you do it then."

He said, "Good I just did."

I said, "That sounds great."

PATTY. He said, "Excellent I'll talk to you later."

I said, "Okay bye."

CHET. *(To* **LARRY.***)* He sounds intense.

PATTY. Our futures sit in the balance here gentlemen.

Now we got like ten minutes to come up with something credible to give 'em, so what do we got?

LARRY. Well, Patty it's not like we can just make something up, we checked all the addresses on the list.

CHET. Yeah, all three.

LARRY. You know?

CHET. All of 'em.

LARRY. I mean, it's definitely not Joyce Verdi. You know. She's got that diseased foot thing going on. So / she's not –

CHET. It looks *real* weird.

LARRY. And – right. So she's not driving around right now, so it's not her.

And then Freddy Young, his wife was using the car at work all last night.

CHET. Which we confirmed.

PATTY. And the third place?

LARRY. Oh. Uh…you don't need to worry about that place.

PATTY. *(Eyes narrowing.)* Why?

LARRY. No, just – it's Llewanne Womack's place. I don't know if you (know her).

Megan's best friends with her granddaughter. And they were over there last night. So…you know.

PATTY. Your daughter…

LARRY. Yeah.

PATTY. ...Your *teenage* daughter.

LARRY. Yeah.

PATTY. With her *teenage* friend.

LARRY. ...Yeah?

PATTY. And since it is two teenage girls we're lookin' for here, I can't see why that'd raise ANY, RED, FLAGS.

(Short pause.)

LARRY. *(Finally realizing what she's saying.)* Whoa, hey, Patty –

PATTY. Jesus Christ, Larry.

LARRY. Hey, hey, Megan would never do something like that. Okay? She is a very nice, well-behaved, nice young woman.

She may be going through a rough patch, okay, for a couple a' years. A couple year rough patch, but she always has super good intentions.

CHET. Yeah, we talked to her when we were there. She was totally nice and cheerful.

PATTY. This is the same girl that set her school on fire two different times.

LARRY. *Accidentally.*

PATTY. *Both times?*

LARRY. *(Getting flustered.)* You know, I – look. If you really must know. She was over there because she was making my birthday present.

A surprise birthday present.

Okay?

So.

You know.

LARRY. Thank you and all for the accusations. But she was trying to do a super super kind thing. Because she's a really kind person. And sometimes people deserve the benefit of the doubt. I'm sure you'd feel the same way about your sons. About Jason and Jarrett.

(The office phone starts ringing.)

CHET. *(Answering the phone.)* Nine-one-one, this is Chet speaking.

PATTY. I swear to God sometimes Larry, it's like you're waitin' for the criminals to walk up and say, "We're the criminals!"

CHET. *(Placing hand over phone.)* Guys guys guys –

There's a ten-year-old on the phone who wants to report a kidnapping.

(Beat while everyone looks at each other.)

PATTY. Speakerphone speakerphone speakerphone.

CHET. She asked for Larry.

*(**CHET** hits the speakerphone.)*

LARRY. This is Officer Larry McClasky, who am I speaking with?

KIMMY. *(Voice.)* Mr. McClasky? It's Kimmy.

LARRY. Kimberly? What's wrong?

KIMMY. *(Voice.)* Um. I don't know how to tell you this?

But... *(Upset.)* I think I lost Megan.

LARRY. What do you mean you think you – you what? What happened?

KIMMY. *(Voice.)* Please don't tell her I told you this? But we might've went to the Rick Montgomery concert last night?

LARRY. I thought y'all were making, um...presents.

KIMMY. *(Voice.)* What? No. Why?

LARRY. *(Heartbroken.)* Oh. Uh...nothing

Go on.

KIMMY. *(Voice.)* And so, but – and after it was over, we went over to Mr. Montgomery's trailer to say hello?

And then he came back to my house to hang out for a little while?

And then he ended up being really really rude to us?

And he drove off with Megan ten minutes ago.

LARRY. He WHAT?!

KIMMY. *(Voice.)* Yeah. He said he's taking her to his house.

LARRY. He took my daughter?!

PATTY. Whoa whoa whoa whoa whoa. Let's slow down for a second.

Back to the beginning... How did you say you got Mr. Montgomery back to your house again?

KIMMY. *(Voice.)* ...am I on speakerphone?

PATTY. This is Police Chief Patricia Peterson. I'm gonna need you to tell me about the events that transpired in getting Mr. Montgomery back to your residential address.

KIMMY. *(Voice.)* Um. I was actually

Can I just talk to Mr. McClasky?

PATTY. Young lady this is official Sheepshead County Police Department business now, so I'm gonna need you to answer the question.

KIMMY. *(Voice.)* We...invited him?

PATTY. Why?

KIMMY. *(Voice.)* To...hang out in my bedroom and sing songs and stuff?

PATTY. "Sing songs and stuff"?

LARRY. And then what happened?! What's she doing with him? Where'd he take her?

PATTY. Larry.

LARRY. Where's he taken her, you said it was his house?

PATTY. Larry!

LARRY. What did he say he was gonna do with her, what'd / he say –

PATTY. Officer McClasky!

(He shuts up.)

Now. Kimberly is it?

KIMMY. *(Voice.)* Yes ma'am?

PATTY. You happen to have the address of this house?

KIMMY. *(Voice.)* Um. He said it was a couple hours down I-10 West. They just left in my grandma's car.

(Quiet.) They didn't even ask if they could use it.

PATTY. Alright, here's what we're gonna do. I'm gonna need you to stay put because I'm sendin' officers McClasky and Walker out to pick you up and bring you to the station. Understand?

KIMMY. *(Voice.)* Wh-what?

PATTY. We're gonna have to file a complete report. Now I'm gonna hand you off to Officer Walker.

*(She hands the phone over to **CHET**.)*

CHET. *(Into the phone.)* This is Officer Walker.

LARRY. Patty I don't have time to go pick her up. I'm on my way to get Megan right now.

PATTY. No. You're not, Larry.

You're gonna grab Chet.

Get in your police cruiser.

And go pick up that young girl.

LARRY. We'll lose valuable time. We gotta send someone after them now!

PATTY. Never said I wasn't sendin' someone.

Chet. Go to the office. And bring me my belt and hat.

CHET. …I'm on the phone.

PATTY. Get the belt and hat, Chet!

CHET. *(Into the phone.)* I'm gonna have to put you on hold for a second.

LARRY. What are you doin'?

PATTY. Already had your shot, Larry.

You missed.

LARRY. I missed?

PATTY. Besides you're too close to the situation and the people involved.

Can't let your emotions fuck this whole thing up for all of us.

LARRY. I won't let my emotions screw it up though! I won't!

PATTY. That's a sweet thought.

LARRY. Patty, come on! This is me here. It's *me*. You know? Let me do this!

PATTY. Look, you're a nice enough guy Larry.

Nobody really complains about you.

Shit, most people actually like you.

But you're not reliable. Alright?

I mean, you're reliable for most things, but

Out in the field? You just…

You're a desk cop.

You know?

You're the guy who's really good at filing reports. And making sure the break room is stocked.

Now, there's nothing wrong with that. It's not a bad thing.

But that's what you are.

You're not the guy who goes and gets the bad guy.

> (**LARRY** *looks like he's about to stand up for himself. Then chickens out.*)

LARRY. Tell Chet I'll be in the car.

> (*And he sulks out.* **CHET** *walks up with Patty's belt and hat. He's been watching.*)

CHET. He's right, you know. He *would* do a good job.

PATTY. I'm sure he would try.

CHET. Just bring her back safe, okay?

PATTY. What. You think I believed all that bullshit that little girl was sayin'?

I'm not going after Rick… I'm going after Megan.

CHET. And you're not gonna let Larry do it??

PATTY. Being a good dad doesn't make you a good cop.

CHET. It could. In this case it could!

You don't see what I see. When we're out there on the road? He would do anything for her!

And that's just – that's not like a given, you know?

When you're growing up? To have that person that would do that for you?

Not everyone gets that.

That's actually like a totally rare thing!

So when you see someone that cares about their kid that much?

Who cares so much that they cry like way more than normal people.

It's so bright? It's so bright and magical?

It's like staring directly into the sun!

PATTY. I think maybe you should get a new mentor Chet.

CHET. I think maybe *you* should get a new mentor!

PATTY. Excuse / me?

CHET. 'Cause he's gonna rise up!

You guys may laugh at him in the break room?

But that guy is a *volcano*!!

He's been lying dormant for all these years but now is his time, so take a look!

'Cause that guy is about to erupt like Mount freaking Rushmore!

(Blackout.)

Scene Eight

> (**RICK** and **MEGAN** *are in Kimmy's grandma's car.* **RICK** *is driving with* **MEGAN** *riding shotgun.*)
>
> (*They drive in silence for a little while.*)

RICK. Okay.

I feel like one of us should say something 'cause this is getting weird.

> (*Short pause.*)

And I really don't want it to be me.

MEGAN. We don't need to talk.

> (**RICK** *looks at her. Fuck, no, they have to talk.*)

RICK. How'd you even find me?

MEGAN. I go to school with the girl who works reception at the adoption agency.

I fake cried for like thirty minutes and bought her a bag of Cheetos.

RICK. *(Respect.)* ...Nice.

> (**MEGAN** *doesn't want to say thank you.*)

And "kidnapping people." Is that like a new extracurricular you're doing these days, or?

MEGAN. *(That's stupid.)* Extracurricular?

RICK. Yeah, what kind of a thirteen-year-old goes around in / a ski mask –

MEGAN. I'm fourteen.

RICK. Fourteen. / Fine –

MEGAN. *Dumbass.*

RICK. *Fine.*

MEGAN. And I wasn't *trying* to kidnap you.

RICK. Oh! Well. Congratulations on your plan then.

MEGAN. Thank you.

RICK. I'm sure your parents are proud.

MEGAN. Woooow.

RICK. Do they know about this?

Is this like, they're okay with / this?

MEGAN. Okay. *Dude?!*

We really don't need to talk.

(Pause.)

RICK. If you'd really wanted the guitar you could've just emailed me you know.

MEGAN. Emailed you.

RICK. Or whatever. You didn't have to, you know, punch me and smash my fingers.

Would've saved us both a lot of trouble.

MEGAN. Yeah. I'm sure you would've responded.

RICK. …Fair.

(Pause.)

I guess you're wanting some kind of explanation, right?

MEGAN. …

RICK. Or maybe not.

MEGAN. …

RICK. Look.

Let's just say...however your life's turned out? Even with all this shit tonight? You were better off.

I mean / we were –

MEGAN. Do you even know Brenda and Larry?

RICK. I'm pretty certain they're better than we / would've been.

MEGAN. Do you know them?

RICK. No...we didn't want to be involved in the adoption process.

MEGAN. Great. Well you gave me to assholes.

Just by the way.

Just in case you wanted to know.

Y'all gave me to a couple of assholes.

RICK. Oh please. All kids think their parents are assholes.

MEGAN. They're not my parents.

RICK. Then what are they?

MEGAN. ...

RICK. *(It dawns on him.)* Ahhhh, okay.

MEGAN. What?

RICK. I get it.

MEGAN. *What?*

RICK. Why you need that $20,000 so bad.

You're running away.

MEGAN. I never said that.

RICK. Shit. It's what I would do.

It's what I *did*.

MEGAN. When?

RICK. Your age, probably. A little older.

In which case, I'm just gonna say it… if you think this right here is like, some kinda *reunion*? / Some kinda –

MEGAN. Oh my God.

RICK. – father-daughter getaway escape thing where I help you? Let me just put that to bed real quick.

MEGAN. Don't even flatter yourself dude.

I am *not* trying to do anything with you.

(Physically shudders.) Yuhgh.

RICK. Good.

    (Short pause.)

Although I have to say. Running away doesn't solve the problems you think it's going / to solve.

MEGAN. I'm sorry. Do you even know what it's like – do you have any idea

To grow up with these two people

That are so like

Fucking

    (Makes a sound from her gut like uuuuuggghhh.)

Weak.

…

Smiling all the time.

Acting like everything is fucking pancakes.

Fish Taco nights.

All the while, *neither* of them has the backbone to confront even ONE of their problems.

MEGAN. *Everyone* thinks we're losers, *everyone*.

It's like, stop going fishing every other weekend Larry, pretending you had an awesome time while you know Brenda's at home cheating on you with fucking Alan, her boss.

I mean the guy's name is *Alan*!

He's a dentist!

You're a cop dude, you own a gun, you should fucking kill that guy!

Not invite him over for dinner and let him eat at your table.

At your TABLE?

My freshman year, I set a small fire in my chemistry class to get out of taking a test. And Larry convinced everyone it was an accident, so I didn't get in trouble.

I did it again second semester. And Larry told everyone it was an accident. Again.

Two accidents?

Really Larry?!

Come ON dude!

Stop being so fucking WEAK all the time!

And to think that *every* day since you can remember.

And then! All of a sudden! When you're twelve you find out: whoops! Actually we're not your parents.

Nope.

We're just like, other people.

To find that out after all that time. After all those years. And be like: FUCK yes. I KNEW it.

My *real* parents are probably like

Like

NASA people.

They're probably like *spies*.

And then to cry on this stupid girl's shoulder for half an hour just to get the files, open up the envelope, look inside and find out that your real parents are…

(Disgust.) Country singers?

Fucking *country singers*?

…

Awesome.

RICK. "Oohhhh, my parents aren't perfect, my mom's cheating on my dad."

Get over it.

My dad was an accountant.

Think about *that*.

MEGAN. I don't even know what that means.

RICK. Running away from it all's not gonna help you.

MEGAN. It helped you.

RICK. Running away from my parents didn't solve anything.

MEGAN. I'm not talking about your parents.

(He looks at her.)

RICK. Yeah, well.

It'll probably make you happy to know that leaving you at the hospital that day's caused me nothing but a goddamn ocean of grief and nonsense ever since.

I mean it was okay for a couple years.

But then…*every* year. At the same. Mary started waking up in the middle of the night.

RICK. She'd have a "dream" or something that you were in trouble.

Or you died.

Or you were in jail. What the fuck a five-year-old is doing in jail is, you know.

I'd catch her wandering off sometimes.

Sitting in the parking lots of schools.

Buying kids breakfast cereal.

Looking at missing girls posters online.

Just...worrying.

Worrying worrying worrying.

Mostly though.

Worried she'd never get to meet you.

I tried telling her she didn't need to worry about that. But.

Mary was gonna do what Mary was gonna do.

(Beat.)

MEGAN. Wow...

RICK. She was a pretty stubborn person.

MEGAN. That must've been hard.

RICK. Yeah, well.

MEGAN. No, seriously.

That must've been really hard, for her.

To have to worry so much.

RICK. *(Take it easy.)* Okay.

MEGAN. I'm just glad she doesn't have to deal with that anymore. I mean, if she had kept that up, she might've worried herself to death! That would've been terrible!

Thank God that's out of the way, right?

> (**RICK** *starts to turn the steering wheel.*)

What are you doing?

> (*He stops the car.*)

Why are you pulling over?

> (**RICK** *suddenly grabs* **MEGAN**'s *face, not angrily, but very purposefully.* **MEGAN** *drops her hammer and struggles.*)

(Muffled.) What are you doing?! Stop! What are you –

RICK. *(Calmly.)* Shhhhhhhhh.

…

Now.

You can be as mad as you want at me.

But that's my best friend that just died.

> (*He pauses for a moment. Then gets back to his story, without taking his hand off her face.*)

As I was saying.

She used to worry she'd never meet you.

And I'd tell her.

If she's really your daughter, you don't need to worry, because she will find you herself.

She will not let this wrong that we've done her stand.

If she's truly your daughter?

She will seek out her vengeance and lay it at our doorstep with the fury of a spurned god.

And make sure that we never forget about her again.

(He removes his hand.)

RICK. ...And here you are.

(Pause.)

I'm sorry we fucked you over. I am.

But don't misunderstand me.

I'm not doing this for you. This for Mary. She'd want you to have her guitar.

You wanna keep it? You wanna sell it?

That's up to you.

MEGAN. Good.

Then don't misunderstand me.

Because I don't want to have it.

And I don't want to sell it.

...

I want to *destroy* it.

I want to take it out of its case.

Bring it into the woods.

And just go fucking, crazy on it.

And after I'm done smashing it, I'm gonna build a bonfire.

And take all of those tiny tiny pieces that are left.

And *burn* them.

And then.

After the fire goes out.

I'm gonna take the ashes.

And I'm gonna burn those.

I'm gonna burn 'em until the ashes turn to dust.

And the dust breaks apart into atoms.

And the atoms dissolve into nothing.

And the protons and electrons and neutrons fly off and get lost and *die*.

And then the universe forgets it, and my mom, and my grandma, and her grandma ever existed.

(Pause. She looks at **RICK**.*)*

I don't care if she worried.

If she got to forget that I existed.

It's only fair that the universe forgets she existed too.

(Blackout.)

Scene Ten

(**LARRY** and **CHET** are riding in the police cruiser. **KIMMY**'s sitting in the back seat.)

(**CHET** turns his camera around so that it's pointed at him.)

CHET. *(Hushed tone.)* Okay. So we are here in the cruiser driving back to the police station after having just picked up an underage female suspect.

(**KIMMY** looks at him. What?)

Once we get back to the station, Officer McClasky and I are gonna work on bringing this case home for a landing.

And then the Chief's gonna come back with Megan and Mr. Montgomery. / And we're –

LARRY. Chet turn it off.

CHET. I'm trying to set the scene man. Context. You gotta give the audience context / for what they're –

LARRY. Just turn it off.

CHET. Like…for good? Or…

(**LARRY** doesn't respond. **CHET** turns it off.)

KIMMY. What do you mean "when the Chief comes back with Megan"?

LARRY. We'll talk about it when we get back to the station.

CHET. She went after them herself.

KIMMY. *(To **LARRY**.)* No but – I thought *you* were gonna go after them.

LARRY. We'll talk about it at the station, Kimberly. We gotta get it all on record.

KIMMY. But…you're her dad.

LARRY. Kimberly –

KIMMY. That's what dads do. They go out and they tell their kids they shouldn't have gotten in the car with the country music star without telling their best friend what they were doing.

CHET. Is that what happened?

KIMMY. That's what I'm saying. I don't know. I don't know what she's doing!

LARRY. Look, Patty wants to take care of it, so – and it's her, you know, prerogative. So that's the end of it. It'll be fine.

KIMMY. Is this 'cause of that incident?

    (They both look at her.)

Or – sorry.

LARRY. Megan told you about that?

KIMMY. No. Just…things I heard at school.

LARRY. You heard that at school?!

    *(**CHET** shakes his head like "no" at her.)*

KIMMY. I mean…n-nooooooo. I don't know. Maybe.

LARRY. Oh Jesus…

CHET. Hey come on man, it's just –

    *(To **KIMMY**.)* You know what? Whatever those kids said, whatever they said, they *lied*. Alright?

KIMMY. *(Quiet.)* It's also on YouTube…

CHET. *(Absolutely serious throughout.)* Yeah well you know what? Whatever that video said, it *lied*. Alright?

He was saving those people in that McDonald's.

That's what he was doing.

You know this is what people don't understand.

When a guy has his hand in a McDonald's bag and says there's a gun in there, you just don't know. You know?

It could be anything in there!

A gun. A shotgun. A knife.

You ever seen a McDonald's bag? They're huge!

A machete? It could be anything!

And also. *Also*.

The reason he was totally cooperating and like,

When he got down on his hands and knees, instead of "pulling his firearm" –

'Cause that's an easy thing to just do –

Is 'cause he was trying to protect all those people in there from harm!

He was diffusing the situation!

That's why he gave him the keys to our old cruiser. He was trying to get the guy out of there.

That's what a freaking cop of the *law* does! You know?

He puts himself on the line.

Without worrying about like, humiliation or embarrassment and takes one for the people around him.

And everyone's shitting on him about it, and making fun, when they have no idea.

They have NO idea.

I mean you're looking at a savior here!

He's a selfless savior!

LARRY. He didn't have a gun.

(Tiny pause.)

CHET. What?

LARRY. He didn't have a gun.

CHET. Yes he did. That's what everyone / was –

LARRY. No he didn't.

CHET. Aw come on man, you don't know that –

LARRY. He was wearin' *a bag on his hand* Chet. Of course he – come on!

CHET. Dude what're you talking about?

LARRY. You don't have to be a freakin' scientist to – you know?!

CHET. No man, don't start spiraling / okay?

LARRY. I'm *not* spiraling –

CHET. You're only saying that / 'cause you're –

LARRY. 'Cause I was scared!

Okay? I was scared!

Even when I figured out he didn't actually have a gun, I still didn't get off the ground.

I just...laid there.

CHET. Nah man, you weren't scared!

LARRY. No Chet –

CHET. You were savin' those people.

Savin' all of 'em!

LARRY. No I wasn't.

CHET. Nah, come on man, you're a superstar!

LARRY. Stop / Chet.

CHET. You're the fucking King Kong of cops man!

LARRY. STOP CHET!

CHET. Why, I'm / serious!

LARRY. 'CAUSE I'M A LOSER, MAN!

Alright?!

>   *(Starts crying.)*

I'm a fuckin' loser.

I'm a desk cop, man!

I'm scared.

I wake up every morning and I'm just scared

And I don't know what to do.

I don't know what I'm doing anymore.

And everyone can see it.

When I look in their eyes?

Brenda sees it.

Everyone at work.

Even Megan.

They think I'm *nothing*.

I'm not a cop.

I'm not even a real dad.

I'm a fuckin' loser, man.

>   *(Long pause.)*

KIMMY. That's not true.

LARRY. *(Just remembering she's back there.)* Ahhhh. I'm sorry.

You shouldn't –

(Clears his eyes.)

You shouldn't be seein' this.

KIMMY. Megan doesn't think that.

You're the only one she'll actually listen to.

That's why I was calling *you*. Not the police. I called *you*.

'Cause you keep her safe.

Like the first time she set the school on fire and you came and told her stop?

She listened to you.

And the second time she set the school on fire and you told her stop again?

She listened to you.

When we're together?

And we're about to do something dangerous? She always looks at me directly in the eyes and says, "Don't tell Larry." Not her mom. Not our teachers. She says *Larry*. And she means it.

LARRY. ...Yeah?

KIMMY. And I don't care who the Chief is. I know Megan'd want you to be the one to get rid of Mr. Montgomery.

CHET. Actually, the Chief is going after Megan.

LARRY. She's what?

CHET. I thought she told you. She's pickin' up both of them, but, I think she's gonna arrest Megan.

KIMMY. But that's not fair, she didn't even do anything.

Can she do that?

>   (**LARRY** *darkens.*)

LARRY. No...

No she cannot.

CHET. What?

LARRY. She will not do that!

Everybody put your seat belts on!

CHET. Why?

LARRY. *WE'RE GOIN' TO GET MY DAUGHTER!!*

>   (**LARRY** *hits the siren and does a HARD 180° with the cruiser! Tires squeal! Everybody lurches to the right!)*

LARRY.	**CHET.**	**KIMMY.**
AAAAAAAAAAAHHHHHHH!!	WHOA WHAT! WHAT!	AAAAAAAHHHHHHHHH!!

Scene Eleven

(The inside of a gas station. The part with all the snacks and condoms and where you pay for gas. **RICK** *enters, followed by* **MEGAN**.*)*

RICK. You can stay in the car.

MEGAN. Yeah. 'Cause I'm some asshole who's gonna let you out of my sight.

RICK. *(Annoyed.)* Jesus. Fine.

MEGAN. Fine!

RICK. You want anything? *(Re: snacks.)*

MEGAN. Um. *No?*

RICK. Okay suit yourself.

> *(He starts to walk to the register.)*

MEGAN. Wait.

(Quiet.) ...Doritos.

> *(He grabs Cool Ranch Doritos.*)*

(Quiet.) Nacho Cheese.

> *(***RICK*** puts Cool Ranch back. Grabs Nacho Cheese. Then walks up to the register. But there's nobody there.)*

RICK. Hello?

> *(***PATTY*** walks in! Meaning business. She eyes* ***RICK****. He notices. She sees* ***MEGAN****.)*

PATTY. Megan.

---

* A license to produce *Country Girls* does not include a license to publicly display any branded logos or trademarked images. Licensees must acquire rights for any logos and/or images or create their own.

MEGAN. *(Under her breath.)* Oh shit.

RICK. What's goin' on Sheriff?

PATTY. Are you Rick Montgomery?

RICK. It's possible... Why?

PATTY. *(Huge sigh of relief.)* Hooooo.

Son. Have I got some people who're gonna be glad to see you.

RICK. What?

PATTY. You're safe now. You understand? *You're safe.*

I've been sent here to retrieve you.

Now. I got your good friend the Governor on speed dial. He's been goin' crazy about your whereabouts for the past sixteen hours. Why don't you step outside and stand by my car. I'll be right out after dealing with this one here.

MEGAN. What? I didn't do anything.

PATTY. Oh, come now. Let's not do that.

You know what you've done.

MEGAN. I think you should talk to my dad.

I'm sure he'd be very interested to hear that you're throwing accusations, *false* accusations at me.

PATTY. Your dad already knows. Why do you think I'm here?

MEGAN. ...What?

PATTY. Now. Drop the hammer, and walk towards me slowly, with your hands raised.

RICK. Whoa okay okay. Officer?

PATTY. Police Chief Patricia Peterson.

RICK. I – Police Chief Peterson. Ma'am. I think maybe there's been some kinda, miscommunication here.

PATTY. Miscommunication…

RICK. I don't know what you heard, but…I'm not sure this girl's done all that you think she's done.

PATTY. Oh, okay, okay.

So are you talking about the kidnapping, the breaking and entering, trespassing, theft, or destruction of property?

Which one of those was there a miscommunication on?

Or maybe I should add assault now I'm looking at you. What the hell happened to your face?

RICK. I fell.

PATTY. Yeah.

*(Looks at **MEGAN**.)*

I bet you fucking fell.

RICK. Look. We're on our way somewhere right now. So maybe there's some way we can work this out.

PATTY. …Work it out?

RICK. Yeah. Like make a little exchange or something.

PATTY. Excuse me?

RICK. Like maybe there's something you need.

Or something you want. That you don't have. That I could provide.

PATTY. Are you having a li'l bit of a break from reality right now, son?

RICK. It's like you said, I've got this phone call I've gotta make to my, good friend, the Governor.

And that phone call can go one of two ways.

RICK. It can either go "Hey Greg, how's it going? Oh not much, just feelin' safe and secure thanks to the fine efforts of the lovely Chief Peterson here. A woman you might think about givin' a hard look at for the next State Police Commissioner. She's such a kind and accommodating and understanding person."

Or...I can make a very different kinda phone call.

So here's what I'm gonna do.

I'm gonna count to three.

And by the time I get there, you're gonna have turned around. Walked out the store. And gone back to your car.

*(Slight pause. **PATTY** looks at both of them.)*

PATTY. I'm sorry. But who exactly do you think you're having a conversation with here?

Look at the hat.

Check out the gun.

I am a forty-five-year-old American woman. I've been divorced three times, given birth to two dipshits, been stabbed one time, and have fucked up exactly zero arrests.

I am the Goddamn Law, son.

Now I don't know what kinda fucked up shit y'all are getting up to, but y'all are coming with me.

*(**PATTY** draws her gun. But doesn't point it at them.)*

RICK. One. Two.

PATTY. Ooooh boy. You do not want to get to –

RICK. Three.

(**CHET** *busts in the gas station.*)

CHET. Chief! We saw your car outside!

PATTY. Chet, WHAT?! You're supposed to pick up that girl.

CHET. No it's cool, we brought her.

PATTY. You *what?!*

(**KIMMY** *and* **LARRY** *bust in. He's already super emotional and out of breath.*)

LARRY. *SWEETHEART?!*

PATTY. GODDAMN IT LARRY!

LARRY. *(Seeing* **MEGAN**.*)* Oh thank God! Oh thank God.

PATTY. You're supposed to be at the station with *her*!

LARRY. Sorry Patty!

(*Shouting for some reason.*) Sweetheart? Are you okay?

MEGAN. Kimmy, did you...*tell them* what I was doing??

KIMMY. I'm so sorry it's not my fault I just love you.

LARRY. *(Just, like, shouting.)* Dad's gonna take care of it, okay?! Stay right there!!

PATTY. Larry, I have this under control.

Now take Chet. Get in your vehicle. And drive the hell back to the station. *Now.*

(*Brief pause.* **LARRY** *notices* **PATTY**'s *gun.*)

LARRY. Patty why's your gun out.

PATTY. Did you hear what I said?

LARRY. Why's your gun out, Patty?

PATTY. Because I'm in the middle of an arrest right here. *In case you / noticed.*

LARRY. That's my daughter over there! You can't just / be –

PATTY. And she broke the law! That's sorta the way it works!

LARRY. Patty you put that thing up right now!!

>   (**LARRY** *puts his hand on his gun.*)

PATTY. Or what, Larry?

LARRY. *(Warning.)* Patricia.

PATTY. *Or what, Larry?*

>   (**LARRY** *draws his gun, but keeps it pointed at the floor.*)

LARRY. I don't wanna do this Patty don't make me do this.

PATTY. Don't point your gun at me Larry!

LARRY. I'm not I'm just holdin' it.

PATTY. You're pointin' it at me.

LARRY. I'm not pointin' it I'm pointin' at the floor –

PATTY. You're pointin' it in my direction –

LARRY. Stop bringing your gun up!

PATTY. *You* stop bringing your gun up –

LARRY. I'm not bringing it up you're bringing it up stop bringing it up, Patty!

PATTY.	**LARRY.**
Drop the gun Larry, you are in major breach of –	You're making me do it, I don't want to!
Lower the gun right now!	You lower it!
Lower it!	*You* lower it!
I swear to God!	I don't wanna do this!
Lower it!	Stop making me do this!

I'm not making you do anything you're the one who's supposed to lower yourgunnotmethisismy jurisaaaaaaaaaaaaaaaaa aaaaaaaaaahhhhhhAAA AAAAAAAAAAAAAAAA AAAAAAAAAAHHHH HHHHHHHHHHHHH HHHHHHHH!!!!!!!!!! !!!!!!!!!!!!!!!!!!!!!!!!!!!!! !!!!!!!!!!!!!!!!!

Patty lower your gun so I can lower my gun Idon'twannahavemygun upaaaaaaaaaaaaaaaaaaaa aaAAAAAAAAAAAAAA AAAAAAAAAAAAAAA AAAAAAAAHHHHHH HHHHHHHHHHHHH HHHHHHHHHHHHH HHHHHHHHHHHHH HHHHHH!!!!!!!!!!!!!!! !!!!!!!!!!!!!!!!!!!!!!!!!!!!! !!!!!!!!!!!!!!!!

(They're both totally pointing their guns at each other right now.)

CHET. *(Total calm.)* Hey guys? We're in a *gas station*. Um.

LARRY. You're not taking my daughter Patty.

PATTY. It's not your call to make.

LARRY. Yes it is! She has been tricked. And abducted. By a country music star.

So I am taking *him* back to the station. And taking *her* home.

MEGAN. You can't!

LARRY. I'm taking care of it sweetheart!

MEGAN. He didn't trick me!

LARRY. It's okay, you don't know what you're saying right now.

MEGAN. He didn't trick me, he's my dad!

(Everything stops.)

LARRY. Wh...what?

MEGAN. ...He's my dad.

PATTY. ...Holy shit balls. **CHET.** Whoa. **KIMMY.** *What*??

LARRY. *(To* **RICK.***)* Is that, true?

RICK. ...Yeah.

LARRY. Oh... Oh... Okay.

Wow. Uh... I don't really know what to do with myself right now.

RICK. Look, it's alright. But right now, we gotta –

> *(BANG!* **LARRY***'s gun goes off. The freezer behind* **MEGAN** *and* **RICK** *explodes.)*

WHOA! WHOA! OKAY!

LARRY. Oh my God. Megan?!

RICK. Let's everyone put their guns away right now!

LARRY. I'm so sorry.

RICK. *(To* **MEGAN.***)* Are you alright?

MEGAN. What?

RICK. *(To* **MEGAN.***)* You're okay?

> *(***MEGAN** *nods to* **RICK.***)*

Alright. This girl and me are on a trip right now.

And considering that all y'all are doing is fucking endangering people

I'm going to make a goddamn executive decision and take this girl outta here with me.

PATTY. We can't let you do that.

I realize what just happened was real fucked up but we cannot let you do that.

RICK. Y'all got those bodycams, right?

You want this whole thing getting reported? Getting out on the internet?

Sheepshead County Police Department almost shoots innocent people?

> (**PATTY** *doesn't respond.*)

I didn't think so.

LARRY. Megan. What are you doing?

MEGAN. *(Stops to look at him for a moment.)* ...Sorry Larry.

> (**RICK** *and* **MEGAN** *leave the gas station.*)

Scene Twelve

(**MEGAN** and **RICK** *are driving. Fast.* **RICK** *in the driver's seat,* **MEGAN** *as passenger.*)

MEGAN. What the hell was that dude?

RICK. What?

MEGAN. I don't need you like, fucking, saving me or whatever that was.

RICK. I wasn't.

MEGAN. Asking me if I'm alright?

RICK. What?

MEGAN. Don't do that shit!

RICK. Uh. There was a gunshot!

Sorry. Jesus.

MEGAN. Well whatever!

I'm fine.

You don't need to like –

(**RICK** *suddenly passes out and falls over into* **MEGAN**. *He swerves the car.*)

WHOA! What the hell!!

RICK. *(Waking up.)* Aaaahhhwhat?

MEGAN. You just passed out!

RICK. *(Nauseous.)* Whoa...

MEGAN. What's wrong with you!?

(**RICK** *pats up and down his body. Down to his legs. His hand comes away bloody.*)

Did you get shot?!

RICK. Aw man. I think I got shot.

MEGAN. You *think*??

How do you not know?!

RICK. I don't know! I didn't feel anythsoho–

(He starts to pass out again.)

MEGAN. Oh Jesus Christ. Pull over! Pull over!

(He pulls the car over.)

Quick, let me see your leg.

RICK. What?

MEGAN. GIVE ME YOUR LEG!

*(**RICK** maneuvers his leg around and puts it in **MEGAN**'s lap.)*

RICK. It's fine, it's probably just from the glass.

MEGAN. No, you got shot dude!

RICK. I didn't get shot.

*(**MEGAN** rips open his jeans and blood shoots out all over her and **RICK**.)*

MEGAN.	**RICK.**
WHOOOOOOOAAAAAAWHATTHEFUCK?	OH MY GOD!

MEGAN. Okay. We need to go to the hospital.

RICK. No.

MEGAN. What!

RICK. No. It's fine.

MEGAN. Ummmmmm pretty sure you're literally about to die.

So I'm gonna bring you to the hospital.

RICK. You can't take me to the hospital.

You take me to the hospital and the rest of the world'll catch up to us.

And everything'll get way more complicated.

We need to finish this now.

Here just – we're almost there. Five minutes that way and we're there.

Now just let me DRIVE!

> *(Cut to **KIMMY** standing outside the police cruiser. She looks anxious.)*

CHET. We're getting ready to go.

You okay?

KIMMY. Yeah…

CHET. Are…you sure?

KIMMY. …How do you know if someone's your soul friend or not?

CHET. What?

KIMMY. A soul friend is a –

CHET. Oh no, I know what a soul friend is.

KIMMY. …She didn't tell me that he was her dad.

The only reason you wouldn't tell something like that to your soul friend is if they aren't your real soul friend.

CHET. I don't know.

My niece? Isabelle? She doesn't tell me stuff ALL the time.

KIMMY. But that's your niece.

CHET. Yeah. But she's also like…one of my good best friends.

We go camping together. We blow up dry ice bombs in the woods. It's awesome.

But. She's doing the whole puberty thing right now, so. We haven't really talked for like the past six months.

KIMMY. And that doesn't make it feel like your heart's gonna evaporate?

CHET. No, it does. It does.

But that's what a soul friend does, you just gotta let it evaporate.

Because one day she's gonna call me and be like, "Chet! I'm at school and I need some tampons, help!"

And I'm gonna be like, "okay."

And on that day my heart's gonna feel about as big as the sun.

*(The scene cuts to **PATTY** and **LARRY**. **PATTY**'s just gotten off the phone.)*

PATTY. Alright. I've just pushed the search statewide. We got every county in the state looking for them now. They're also trying to pull up his address.

LARRY. Good. Good.

PATTY. You alright?

LARRY. Uh...yeah? Yeah. I'm okay.

PATTY. Good.

Now. Give me your gun.

LARRY. Aw, Patty...

PATTY. Don't *fucking* "Patty" me, Larry. You pulled your gun on me? And almost shot someone.

Now I know you're going through some shit at the moment? But you do NOT do that.

PATTY. Now: gun.

> (**LARRY** *looks at her. Then slowly hands over his gun.*)

Badge.

> (**LARRY** *hands her his badge.*)

Hat.

> (**LARRY** *hands her his hat.*)

Are you happy with yourself?

> (**LARRY** *looks at his shoes.*)

Jesus Christ Larry. Do you even want to be a cop?

LARRY. ...I don't know.

PATTY. That's the worst answer you could've given.

LARRY. I know.

PATTY. You're done. You understand?

LARRY. Yeah.

PATTY. *But.* Before you go? I need you to look at my face. And apologize.

LARRY. ...Patty –

PATTY. "I'm sorry Patricia. For disobeying direct orders.

For breaking the law.

For almost shooting an innocent bystander.

And for pointing my service weapon at my superior officer."

LARRY. I'm sorry for disobeying orders

And for breaking the law.

And for almost shooting Rick Montgomery.

PATTY. *And I apologize for pointing my service weapon at my superior officer.*

LARRY. Yeah. I don't uh… I don't think I'm gonna do that.

PATTY. Excuse me?

LARRY. I'm not gonna apologize for that.

PATTY. Oh now you're just trying to piss me off.

LARRY. You were pointing a gun at my daughter, Patty. I wasn't doing my job!

PATTY. What?

LARRY. Look, I'm not

I've never been good, at, things.

You know, police work: obviously. School. Brenda's cheating on me with some guy named Alan at Astroworld right now. So that's…you know.

But I'm great at being a father.

That is like…*in my blood.*

I've got dad blood.

So. Yes. I'm sorry you disagree with me on whether Megan is guilty or not. And I'm sorry I disobeyed you. And probably ruined your chances with the Governor.

But I'm not sorry I protected my daughter.

I am the wall that stands between her and those that would do her harm.

*(Pause. Is **PATTY** softening a bit?)*

I'm sure you'd do the same if it was Jason and Jarrett in trouble.

PATTY. Fuck no. Locking those idiots up would be an improvement to their lifestyle.

LARRY. I don't think so.

PATTY. Yeah. Well.

(*Pause.*)

Shit. Here.

(**PATTY** *gives* **LARRY** *his badge back. He looks at her.*)

This isn't me giving you your job back.

But you're gonna need some authority if you're gonna find your daughter.

After that, it's done.

(*He nods.*)

And I'm fuckin' keepin' this, you better believe that shit. (*Re: his gun.*)

Now. Go out there and finish this thing Officer McClasky.

(*He salutes. She salutes back.*)

(*We cut to* **RICK** *and* **MEGAN** *in Rick's home.* **RICK**'s *on the couch. Blood everywhere.* **MEGAN** *is dumping her backpack out on the ground. Everything about this is chaotic.*)

MEGAN. Alright elevate your leg!

RICK. What?

MEGAN. *Elevate your leg!* We need to get the blood flowing in the other direction.

RICK. What the hell are you doing?

MEGAN. I'm gonna seal the wound.

RICK. What does that mean "seal the wound"?

(**MEGAN** *produces a multi-tool from her backpack.*)

WHOA, okay. What – what's going on with that?

MEGAN. It's what I'm gonna use.

RICK. Nope. No. I don't think so.

MEGAN. Come on!

RICK. It's fine.

Just wrap a towel or a shirt around it or something.

MEGAN. Wrap a shirt around it??

RICK. Yeah.

MEGAN. God you're so stupid.

RICK. What are you gonna do?

> (**MEGAN** *grabs the Molotov from her backpack and sanitizes her multi-tool.*)
>
> (*Then she gives it to* **RICK**.)

What's this?

MEGAN. Vodka.

RICK. What do I do with it?

MEGAN. Uh. You're gonna wanna drink like…all of it.

RICK. What?

MEGAN. *Real* quick.

RICK. Why?

MEGAN. And then put this in your mouth.

> (*She gives him a T-shirt from her backpack.*)
>
> (*Then flips a long knife out from her multi-tool.*)

RICK. Wait, what's about to happen?!?

MEGAN. …I'm gonna try to cauterize the wound.

RICK. Whoooaaaa no no no no no.

MEGAN. Come on!

RICK. Nope! Nuh-uh! No!

MEGAN. I have to close the wound, there's no other way!

RICK. Then take me to the hospital.

MEGAN. I thought you said –

RICK. I don't care anymore take me to the hospital! Let the cops come and take you away.

Let 'em take you FAR away from me.

MEGAN. Don't be a baby, it's not gonna be that bad.

RICK. Or let me DIE! I don't care!

MEGAN. Hey!

> *(She slaps him.)*

Don't even joke! Alright?!

If you want to die, *I will let you die.*

But if not you need to man the fuck up in the next three seconds and get ready.

So what's it gonna be?!

> *(Pause. They stare at each other. Then, he puts the T-shirt in his mouth.)*

Okay.

> *(**MEGAN** holds the knife over a lighter, making it super hot.)*

Okay. Okay.

Oh my God.

This is gonna be so fucked up.

Oh my God.

Okay... Ready?

RICK. *(Takes the shirt out of his mouth.)* Wait, wait. Real quick –

> *(He starts reaching for his boot.)*

MEGAN. What do you want?

RICK. In my boot.

> *(**MEGAN** reaches into his boot. Pulls out the little bag of Demerol.)*

MEGAN. How many do you take?

RICK. Like fifteen.

> *(**MEGAN** takes out one pill. Closes the bag, then drops them to the floor. And stomps on them, crushing them.)*

WHAT!? WHY?!

MEGAN. You get *one* more. And that's it.

RICK. Those are my fuckin' pil–

> *(She shoves the shirt back in his mouth and lights her lighter. **RICK** keeps shouting through the shirt.)*

MEGAN. *Don't. Move.*

I've only seen this done on the internet like one time... And it was a grainy video.

RICK. *(Muffled.)* What!

MEGAN. HERE WE GO!!

> *(Annnnnnnd she presses the hot knife against his wound, cauterizing it. Smoke rises from the wound.)*

MEGAN.	**RICK.**
Hooooolyyyyy shiiiiiiiiiiiiiiiiiittttt.	*(Muffled screeeeeeeeeeeam.)*

> (**RICK** *takes the shirt out of his mouth and just starts indiscriminately screaming.*)

RICK. Ahhhhh. Ahhhh. AHHHH.

MEGAN. Are you okay?!?!

RICK. NO!

MEGAN. *(Laughing.)* Oh my God I can't believe that just happened!

RICK. Goddamn it!

MEGAN. *(Still laughing.)* That was so much fun!

RICK. No it was not!!

MEGAN. It smells like steak!

RICK. I hate you!

MEGAN. Awwww, come on.

> *(She takes the T-shirt from him and ties it around his wound. He screams again.)*

Ssshhhhhhh almost done almost done.

How does that feel?

RICK. Terrible.

MEGAN. Don't look at me like that, I just saved your life, idiot.

RICK. Give me my pill.

> (**MEGAN** *holds the pill out to him. He reaches for it, and she pulls it back out of his reach.*)

> (**RICK** *moans in anger/betrayal.*)

MEGAN. Ah-ah. What do we say?

(He stares daggers at her.)

What do we say?

RICK. *(Through gritted teeth.)* Please.

MEGAN. And?

RICK. …Thank you.

MEGAN. Thank you for…?

RICK. Just give me the goddamn pill already Jesus Christ!!

(Pause.)

MEGAN. Thank you forrrrrrr…?

RICK. Thank you for…helping me.

MEGAN. You're welcome.

(She gives him the pill.)

(She opens a bag of Doritos.)

(Decompressing.) Wooo! That was fucking crazy. Want some chips?

RICK. No.

MEGAN. Come on, you should eat.

Seriously. You lost a lot of blood.

(She lays a chip on his chest.)

RICK. I can't remember the last time I had a Dorito.

MEGAN. What?

RICK. I'm a Fritos man.

MEGAN. Gross.

RICK. They're classic.

Doritos always seemed so needy

With all their commercials and different tastes and –

Throwing all kinds of different flavors at you.

It's no good.

You ever see a Fritos commercial?

MEGAN. No?

RICK. Exactly.

They know what they are. They don't need to go telling people about it either.

MEGAN. ...What about Cheetos?

RICK. Who doesn't love Cheetos?

MEGAN. Who doesn't love Cheetos.

> (**MEGAN** *pushes the chip on his chest closer to him.*)

Eat your chip.

> (*He does. They stare at each other for a moment.*)

RICK. Well.

You ready to get to it?

> (**MEGAN** *nods.*)

Bring over that black case in the corner.

> (*She walks across the room and brings back a black guitar case.*)

> (*She sits down by herself. Opens the guitar case. And pulls it out.*)

(…)

(She holds it gently. Like it might break at any moment.)

You ever hear her play?

*(**MEGAN** shakes her head.)*

Not even at a concert?

MEGAN. I always snuck in after.

RICK. You want to?

(…)

She was working on a couple things.

Didn't get to finish them all, so it's not polished, but…

(He grabs a remote, clicks it and the stereo comes to life. He flips through a couple tracks.)

(It starts playing. It's silent for the first little bit. Then we hear background noises.)

*(It's **MARY**'s voice. She's talking to **RICK** in the recording studio. They're mid-conversation.)*

MARY. *(Voiceover.)* Uccggh. One more time.

RICK. *(Voiceover.)* No.

MARY. *(Voiceover.)* Come on. One more.

RICK. *(Voiceover.)* That take was great.

MARY. *(Voiceover.)* Are you stupid?

RICK. *(Voiceover.)* No?

MARY. *(Voiceover.)* That take was terrrrrrible.

RICK. *(Voiceover.)* It was also the sixteenth take.

MARY. *(Voiceover.)* Eighth. *Eighth* take.

RICK. *(Voiceover.)* And they were all great... Come on.

>*(Pause.)*

(Voiceover.) What are you doing?

>*(Pause.)*

(Voiceover.) You're just gonna stand there and pout at me, then?

>*(Pause.)*

(Voiceover.) Pouting's not gonna do anything, go ahead. I'm a stone wall. Pout all night, I got the time.

>*(Pause.)*

(Voiceover.) Ucgh. Fine.

But this is the one. This is it.

MARY. *(Voiceover.)* Yeah, yeah.

RICK. *(Voiceover.)* Take seventeen.

MARY. *(Voiceover.)* Take *nine*.

RICK. *(Voiceover.)* ...Take nine.

>*(Silence. **MARY** clears her throat. More silence. Then: music.)*

>*(It starts out as light strumming.)*

MARY.
> I WISH I HAD KNOWN THE WAY
> I WISH I COULD'VE MADE YOU STAY
> IN A PLACE BEYOND THE FIELDS AND SEA
> A PLACE LIKE MONTGOMERY

> WHERE THE STREETS ARE PAVED FOR YOU
> EVERY MOMENT IS ALWAYS NEW

AND JOY WOULD COME EASILY
BECAUSE YOU'D BE HERE WITH ME

BUT I KNOW I CAN'T GO
BACK YEARS AGO
AND CHANGE OUR HISTORY
I WISH I'D BEEN SMART
I WISH WE'D RESTART
SO I COULD SHOW YOU MONTGOMERY
A PLACE LIKE MONTGOMERY
A PLACE LIKE MONTGOMERY

THE TOWN IS HALF EMPTY NOW
THE LIGHTS ARE DARKER SOMEHOW
WELL, THEY'RE NOT AS BRIGHT AS THEY USED TO BE
I'M NOT SURE IF THAT'S JUST ME

BUT WE'RE STILL HERE AND THERE
ON THE CORNER OF ELMER AND BEAR
AND IF YOU AGREE
PLEASE AGREE
WE COULD TURN THIS TWO INTO THREE

BUT I KNOW IT'S NOT FAIR
TO ASK YOU TO CARE
ABOUT WHAT I WANT OR NEED
BUT DEEP IN MY SOUL
I'D BE MADE WHOLE
IF YOU CAME TO MONTGOMERY
WE'RE HERE IN MONTGOMERY
WE'RE HERE IN MONTGOMERY

BUT I KNOW I CAN'T GO
BACK YEARS AGO
AND CHANGE OUR HISTORY
I WISH I'D BEEN SMART
I WISH WE'D RESTART
'CAUSE I WANT YOU HERE WITH ME
HERE IN MONTGOMERY
HERE IN MONTGOMERY

(She stops playing for a moment. The rest is slow and a cappella.)

MARY.
BUT I KNOW THAT WON'T BE
SOMETHING I'LL SEE
IN THE TIME I HAVE LEFT TO ME

SO I HOPE YOU FIND
A HOME TO CALL MINE
A PLACE LIKE MONTGOMERY

YOUR OWN MONTGOMERY

MY LITTLE MONTGOMERY

*(The songs ends. **MEGAN** and **RICK** are left in the silence.)*

*(**MEGAN** looks at the guitar.)*

*(**MEGAN** gives one of the strings an exploratory pluck. It sounds strange and loud and awkward.)*

(She plucks another string. And then one more. They echo throughout the room.)

(She gives the whole thing a strum.)

(That time sounded good.)

*(**RICK** watches her.)*

(There's a moment.)

(Then...the doorbell rings.)

*(They look up. **MEGAN** looks at **RICK**. Then at the door.)*

(The doorbell rings again.)

LARRY. *(Offstage, yelling.)* Megan?!

MEGAN. Mother*fucker*. They found us.

(The doorbell rings again.)

LARRY. *(Offstage, yelling.)* Hello?!

MEGAN. *Shit.* We gotta get outta here.

> *(She puts the instrument down and starts throwing things back in her backpack.)*

Come on.

RICK. What are you doing?

MEGAN. We can sneak out the back, it's fine.

RICK. We're not going anywhere.

MEGAN. Do you have another car?

RICK. You hear what I said?

> *(She grabs his arm and tries to pull him up.)*

Ow! Stop.

MEGAN. Shut up. Stop whining.

> *(She fails, he falls back on the couch.)*

Come on, you're not even hurt that bad.

RICK. *(Pulling his hand away.)* Stop.

MEGAN. Dude. It's not that hard, they're not that smart of people. Let's go!

RICK. Stop! We're not going anywhere.

MEGAN. Why do you keep saying that?

> *(Pause. She looks at him.)*

Are you giving up?!

RICK. What do you mean giving up? It's not giving up.

I said I'd drive you here and give you that.

That was the deal.

MEGAN. That doesn't mean you have to be a little pussy and like…

RICK. What.

What did you think this was?

MEGAN. This is bullshit!

RICK. Come on. You knew this was always how it was gonna end.

MEGAN. No.

No, you know what?

I'm kidnapping you again!

RICK. Come on.

MEGAN. No, I'm kidnapping you again! Get your shit, let's go.

RICK. I can't stand up.

MEGAN. I DON'T CARE. We're gonna get in the car and go!

RICK. Where?

MEGAN. It doesn't matter. Get your shit!

(He gives her a look.)

I'm not kidding. Let's go!

RICK. Come on.

MEGAN. What!

(He stares at her. Pause.)

…Please?

RICK. It's time.

MEGAN. Please.

*(**RICK** shakes his head.)*

(All of a sudden the loudspeaker from the cruiser outside pops on.)

LARRY. *(Loudspeaker.)* Megan? It's your – it's Larry.

I'm out here with your friend Kimmy.

CHET. *(Muffled/from further away.)* And Chet.

LARRY. *(Loudspeaker.)* Yeah, and Chet. Chet's here as well.

I need y'all to open up the door *right this instant*.

This is not a request!

MEGAN. It's not too late, we could still go out the back.

RICK. And what, keep on running? Have a wild and crazy road trip?

MEGAN. I don't know.

RICK. You think *I'm* wild and crazy?

That man out there shot a person just to protect you.

I'm way too much of a coward to stand in the way of that man.

MEGAN. I hate him though.

RICK. Yeah, well.

We often hate the person we love the most.

MEGAN. I could hate you.

RICK. Nah.

Irritated, maybe. Frustrated, definitely.

But that man outside? You haven't stopped hating on him since we got in the car.

KIMMY. *(Loudspeaker.)* Megan?

(...)

Megan please come outside?

KIMMY. *(Loudspeaker.)* ...I know you might be thinking of sneaking out of the back of the house right now?

And I just wanted to say that I please hope you don't do that.

Because I'm supposed to see you again.

Because we're supposed to live our lives together.

So.

Could you please open the door please?

> *(Pause.)*

RICK. Go on. Open it.

MEGAN. What about you?

RICK. Shit. If you think I have any answers you haven't been paying attention.

Go on. Your people are waiting.

> *(**MEGAN** stares at him. Then turns.)*
>
> *(She walks to the front door. Puts her hand on the knob.)*
>
> *(And opens the door.)*
>
> *(**LARRY**, **CHET**, and **KIMMY** come bursting in and surround **MEGAN** like a family having just found a long lost daughter.)*
>
> *(**LARRY** walks up to her.)*

MEGAN. Hi Larr–

LARRY. *(Shouting.)* DON'T say anything.

You are in SO much trouble!

So much trouble you have no *idea*.

Don't even try to get out of it!

WHY ARE YOU COVERED IN BLOOD?!

OH MY GOD! IS THAT YOUR BLOOD??

MEGAN. No, it's his.

LARRY. OH my God. Oh God.

(To **RICK.***)* What happened to you? Are you okay?!

RICK. Peachy.

LARRY. *(Still shouting.)* That doesn't sound true but okay.

(**CHET** *comes around with his camera.*)

CHET. Look over here! Look over here!

LARRY. NO. This is not a moment Chet!

This is not a commemorative – this is an angry – Larry-is-angry moment!

CHET. Got it.

Woo! Got it! We got the ending!

LARRY. Chet!

Help Mr. Montgomery!

CHET. Hey Rick!

Wow that's a lot of blood!

What happened to you?!

RICK. Just bring me to the hospital.

CHET. You want me to help you to the cruiser?

RICK. Don't touch me.

CHET. You got it man!

I'll bring the cruiser to *you.*

(To **LARRY.***)* I'll bring the cruiser around you guys!!

(**CHET** *sprints out.*)

*(**KIMMY** walks up to **MEGAN**. Holds her hand.)*

KIMMY. I'm really glad you didn't run away. Again.

*(**MEGAN** puts her head on **KIMMY**'s shoulder.)*

LARRY. Hey. Mr., uh, *Rick*.

What happened here?

RICK. I got hurt. And your kid took care of me.

LARRY. She did?

RICK. Yeah.

She's pretty resourceful. And a little dangerous.

LARRY. Yeah.

I've experienced both of those things from her.

Maybe one a little more than the other.

(Slight pause.)

CHET. *(From offstage.)* You guys! I got the cruiser!!

KIMMY. I saved you a seat in the cop car.

LARRY. Kimmy. Would you mind helping Mr. Montgomery outside?

KIMMY. ...Sure.

*(**RICK** wraps an arm around **KIMMY**. She walks him outside. Maybe she makes sure he hits his leg on the door?)*

RICK. Ow.

KIMMY. Oh, was that your leg? I'm so sorry that happened to you...

*(And they're gone. **LARRY** and **MEGAN** are left in the house.)*

LARRY. Megan?

(No response.)

Megan.

MEGAN. Yeah. Sorry.

LARRY. Hey. Whose guitar is that?

MEGAN. Mine… I think.

LARRY. You know how to play?

MEGAN. No.

But I think I could learn.

LARRY. Hmm. Maybe we can try and get you some lessons then.

Or hey, Kimberly could teach you.

MEGAN. Yeah.

LARRY. Maybe y'all could start a band or something.

MEGAN. Maybe.

LARRY. "The Young Banshees." Or uh, uh –

"The Wild Coyotes." You know? That's a pretty cool name, right?

Wild Coyotes?

MEGAN. Yeah.

LARRY. Yeah, y'all should start a band.

…But not for like a YEAR!!

'Cause that's how long you're grounded.

MEGAN. Larry –

LARRY. *(Just making noises.)* NAAHAHHGHAGAH.

Wrong. You. Grounded.

MEGAN. I'm sorry –

LARRY. I realize this is an extraordinary – situation, thing.

But you could've come to me with it.

I would've listened. I am the one who listens. I am the one who helps.

MEGAN. I know.

LARRY. *(Noises again.)* AHAHDAHGAGHAL.

I am the one who takes care of things for you.

Understand?

MEGAN. I said I know.

LARRY. Good…good.

(Pause.)

Hey… He's not going anywhere. You'll see him again.

MEGAN. Yeah?

LARRY. Yeah…

(…)

You wanna take one last look at the place?

MEGAN. No. I'm ready.

(He holds out his hand. She takes it.)

(They walk out together.)

End of Play

Milton Keynes UK
Ingram Content Group UK Ltd.
UKHW022035131124
451149UK00015B/1474

9 780573 710933